# THE ATHENA ALLIANCE

## THE UNDERWORLD SAGA, BOOK FIVE

Eva Pohler

Eva Pohler Books
20011 Park Ranch
San Antonio, Texas 78259
www.evapohler.com

Publisher's Note: This is a work of fiction. Names, characters, places, and incidents are a product of the author's imagination. Locales and public names are sometimes used for atmospheric purposes. Any resemblance to actual people, living or dead, or to businesses, companies, events, institutions, or locales is completely coincidental.

Book Layout ©2017 BookDesignTemplates.com

Book Cover Design by B Rose Designz

The Athena Alliance/ Eva Pohler. -- 1st ed.
Paperback ISBN 978-1-958390-39-9

*For my husband.*

# Contents

# An Unexpected Invitation

Therese leapt into the sky above Mount Ida in the cold snowy air with Ariadne on her heels. Asterion, the Minotaur, hung back, standing beside Thanatos, waiting. The golden disc shot through the clouds, barely missing Helios descending in his cup, before it slowed and spun back toward them.

The disc swung around outside Therese's reach. She and Ariadne both grumbled and turned in the sky to see if Asterion had any better luck. Than and Asterion jumped up from the mountain top at the same time, inches apart, both with determined looks on their faces. The tip of Than's tongue showed between his lips—a habit of his when he was concentrating, which Therese found quite cute. Asterion flew toward the disc with a grunt, but his timing was slightly off, and Than, who'd flown back and to his right, easily caught the disc in one outstretched hand.

"No way!" Therese shouted. She let an arrow fly, aiming close to his ear.

"Watch it!" Than laughed, catching the arrow in one hand, before sending it back to her.

She grabbed it in mock frustration. "Ugh!"

Ariadne rolled her eyes at Therese as the two of them returned to the mountain top. "It's no fun if he always wins."

"We've got to get him, guys," the Minotaur said. "We need to work together."

Than laughed again and shook his head, obviously trying not to gloat. Hip would have already paraded around them twice, but that wasn't Than's style. And yet Therese would feel better if Than did gloat rather than shrugging and looking at them apologetically as though they were a bunch of morons.

Speaking of morons, Therese thought, there was Pete again, bugging her with his prayers. Oh, she shouldn't be so mean. Pete was no moron. He was a kind and good person who had great intentions, and his sister was her best friend. She reminded herself it wasn't that long ago when she'd imagined spending her life with him. Lately, though, his insistence that he relay a message from his father's ghost was really getting on her nerves.

No good thing ever came from knowing the future. She'd learned that lesson after going to the Fates. What they told her hadn't stopped Ares from wanting to imprison her, and it had only made her worry about her future children.

*Two, but none immortal.*

She fingered the locket at her throat.

Than wrapped his arms around her from behind and kissed the back of her neck.

"Your turn," he said. He spun her around to face him and, seeing her frown, asked, "What's wrong?"

"Oh, it's Pete again. He won't let it go."

"Yeah, I know. He's been working on me, too. I've had to block him."

"How do you do that?" she asked.

He touched his finger to the tip of her nose. "Practice, which is what you need with the disc. Now come on."

Like she had much time for practice. Usually she was on Stormy's back flying across the world helping humans and their animal companions. Clifford often went along, and, sometimes, her parents, who lived in the bodies of two immortal red birds, joined her, too. She loved making humans and animals happy and loved spending time with her parents and animal friends, but her duties didn't leave her vast amounts of time for practicing Frisbee throwing. Asterion complained that she and Than didn't come play often enough, but the Minotaur was bound to the Labyrinth and had no other duties but to guard it and so couldn't understand the concept of time management.

"Not all of us can be at many places at once," she said to Than with a wry smile.

Than handed her the disc. Before she could move into position to throw it, Hermes appeared a few feet away. Ariadne and Asterion stepped closer to see what the messenger god had to say.

***

Jen sat up on her bed and threw her pillow in frustration at Pete, who leaned in the doorway of her bedroom. He caught the pillow and threw it back.

"She'll come if you ask her," he said. "Tell her you need a friend—which wouldn't be much of a lie. You barely come out of your room anymore except to do chores."

"And that's exactly why you should quit annoying me," Jen said, throwing her pillow at him again.

He threw it back. "Why won't anyone take me seriously?"

A horrible thought ran through Jen's mind. "You didn't tell Mom or Bobby, did you?"

"Do I look stupid or something?" He sighed. "Of course not. I meant the gods. Than and Therese both ignore me. Hip just sends me sick messages in my dreams. I finally decided to go higher up."

"Higher up?"

"Zeus. Isn't he supposed to be the big shot?"

Jen threw her pillow at his face. "You *are* stupid, Pete! Why would you do such a thing?"

"Why is that so bad? I'm worried about Therese." He tossed the pillow across the room, where it landed on the floor beneath her window. "Why isn't anyone else?"

"I doubt Therese will appreciate you involving Zeus in her problems—though I don't know if he cares, to tell you the truth." She lay back on her pillow-less bed.

"Just ask her to come for a visit," he said again.

"Fine."

When Pete left, Jen crossed the room for her pillow and then sank back on her bed. All she wanted to do these days was sleep. While awake, she only thought of her best friend, who wasn't even human anymore. Or she freaked out over her father's ghost creeping around their place, telling Pete cryptic messages. But while asleep, she could be with Hip. Even when she couldn't sleep, all she had to do was to pray for him to come to her, and he would, and she would instantly drift into a wonderful dream.

She nestled into her covers and called to him. "Hip?"

"Hello, sweetheart," he said in a poor imitation of somebody she recognized but didn't know the name of—some old, classic, long-dead actor. Hip had a habit of doing that. He seriously needed to update his movie references.

But he was dang cute, no matter what he did.

"Hello," she said, stifling a yawn. "Miss me?"

"Always." He sat on her bed.

"When can you come in mortal form so…" she yawned again.

"Soon."

"You always say that." She closed her eyes and gave in to sleep.

***

Hypnos cupped Jen's face in his hands. Even in the Dreamworld, her brown eyes sparkled like those of no other. They were especially sparkly beneath her blond bangs and the full moon and star-filled sky. He and Jen sat beside one another on a moving Ferris wheel. The wind blew his hair into his eyes, so he closed them as he leaned in for a kiss.

She returned his kiss but pulled away earlier than he wanted.

"When?" she asked.

"When what?"

"When will you visit me as a regular guy again?" She narrowed her eyes at him. "Aren't you listening to me?"

He noticed she was getting better and better at transitioning from the waking world to the one of sleep.

"You can continue a conversation from one world to the next?"

"Don't change the subject." She brushed the hair from his eyes.

He didn't know what to say as he bit the inside of his bottom lip. He had no more leverage to abandon his duties and visit her as a mortal man, and unlike his brother, he wasn't willing to risk her life to invite her to become immortal. This meant the only way they could be together was in the world of dreams.

***

Thanatos took Therese's hand as he scrutinized the face of his cousin Hermes. "You don't look like you came to play night Frisbee."

"No. Sorry. Wish I could, though."

"Then why are you here?" Ariadne asked.

Hermes gave them all a smile. "My father wishes to invite you to a party honoring the bride and groom-to-be."

Than and Therese exchanged looks of bewilderment as light flakes of snow dropped around them. Than couldn't help but wonder what Zeus's real motivation was.

"An engagement party," Hermes added. "For you, Than. Therese. Come on, you two." He lifted his palms in front of him as flakes of snow collected on his curly dark beard. "This news was supposed to make you cheerful. The two of you look like you've swallowed a goat."

"You can't blame us for being wary of Zeus," Than said. "Not after what he did to Athena."

"And Cybele," Therese muttered.

"Yes, yes, of course." Hermes waved his hands, as if batting away flies. "But that's all behind us now."

Than wondered how his cousin could say such a thing when Cybele was still missing. Why couldn't Hermes see his father's flaws and stop pandering to his every whim?

Than grimaced as Therese squeezed his hand.

*Ow,* he prayed to her.

*Sorry.* She lightened her grip. *But Hermes acts like attacking the Underworld and kidnapping Athena was nothing. We still don't know what's going on with Cybele.* Her grip tightened once more.

*I know.* Than pulled his hand loose and shook out the cramp.

"Does Zeus really think he can sweep all that under the rug by throwing us a party?" Therese asked.

"Of course." Hermes smiled, showing his teeth.

Therese arched a brow, which Than found sexy. "Will Cybele be there?" she asked.

Hermes's smile faded. "I doubt it."

Therese shook her head and folded her arms across her chest. Than put an arm around her, trying to calm her. She wasn't a volatile person and typically held everything inside, but he worried she might implode one of these days.

"Look, I'm just the messenger," Hermes said. "The engagement party will be held at the winter solstice on Mount Olympus. It's going to be huge."

"But that's right before Christmas," Therese objected. "I'm supposed to be in Colorado. My aunt and uncle are expecting me."

"And it's only a few days away," Than added. "We can't change our plans this late in the game."

"You can do both," Hermes said. "Go to Colorado after my father's party."

"Are we invited?" Asterion asked.

"Of course," Hermes said amiably. "Everyone is."

"Not everyone," Therese murmured.

Than saw she was wearing on his cousin.

"It'll be fun," Hermes added. "My father will make sure of it."

Hermes vanished, leaving the four night-Frisbee players alone in the snow.

A few hours later, Than stood before his hearth gazing at the dancing flames. He couldn't shake the feeling that Zeus's party was more than an attempt to make nice after his attack on Athena and the Underworld a few months ago. He worried Zeus had somehow gotten wind of Athena's plan.

Therese came up behind him and leaned against him, wrapping her arms around his waist. The warmth from her body against him comforted him. Her scent—a mixture of lavender and pine—refreshed him. How had he managed to live for so many centuries without her? He pushed his fingers through hers to link hands, and they stood like that, quietly, for many minutes.

Finally she said, "We can't not show up to Zeus's party when we're the guests of honor."

"Exactly," Than said. "That's what troubles me. What better way to make sure we're there than to make it about us?"

"We're not being overly paranoid, are we?"

He turned to face her. "There's no such thing among the gods." He frowned as he swept her hair from her shoulder and kissed it. "I should have warned you. I didn't make it very clear to you, did I?"

"What are you talking about?"

"When I asked you to join me, among the immortals. You had no way of knowing how intensely dangerous the lives of the gods can be."

She smiled up at him. "I kind of like it. It's exciting."

He smirked. "And to think how bored I was all those centuries before we met."

She moved her lips against his. "Not so boring now, is it?"

He shook his head, brushing her lips softly with his. "Not so much."


The next morning, beneath Larissa Hill, among the ancient water ducts of Lerna, near the Hydra's lair, Thanatos gathered with a handful of gods from the Underworld—his parents, Meg, and Therese—who were joined by Athena, Hephaestus, Apollo, and Artemis. Although the gods could see clearly in the pitch of darkness, a little light filtered in from the outside, and even some of the sounds from the distant city of Argos carried in through the cracks of the heavily warded rock above them. Along with those daytime city sounds came the consistent drip of water, like a slow bass drum, somewhere behind them. The slow tap was mitigated by the flurry of smacks by the Hydra as she enjoyed her cakes.

The gods crowded together in a circle and prayed, rather than spoke, their plans.

*This party by Zeus is suspicious,* Athena agreed after Than had made his concerns known to them.

*You don't think he means to make amends for what he did?* Persephone asked.

Hades turned to the god of truth. *Can you sense what will become of this?*

Apollo shook his head.

*Are you suggesting we move up our plans?* Hephaestus addressed Athena.

Than glanced at Therese, who frowned.

*That would be unwise,* Hades put in.

*I agree,* Athena said. *We've put too much work into these plans to change them now.*

*Drat!* Meg complained. *I was rather excited for a moment there.*

Than rolled his eyes at his sister, who seemed to be too eager for revenge.

*Don't be too eager,* Persephone warned. *There's no guarantee we'll succeed.*

*No,* Artemis agreed. *Especially without Poseidon. I still believe, as I have from the start, that we cannot afford to carry out a plan against Zeus without Earth Shaker.*

*I share my sister's belief,* Apollo said.

*But how can we trust him after what he did to me?* Athena asked, as her face turned red with suppressed rage.

Than agreed with Athena. Poseidon was not to be trusted.

*Let me feel him out,* Apollo suggested. *Of all of us here, I have been his ally most often, and we share a past that has always connected us.*

*You refer to the days after Hera's scheme?* Hades asked.

Than remembered it all too well.

Artemis rested her hands on her knees. *The last attempt to bind Zeus.*

*Which was an utter failure,* Hephaestus added.

*That was then,* Athena said, straightening. *This is now.*

*In any case, I should find out what I can from Poseidon,* Apollo said. *And see if there's hope of winning his alliance for our cause.*

Waste of time, Than thought.

*Poseidon has a soft spot for Therese,* Artemis said. *You might take her with you.*

Than's throat tightened. "What?"

The Hydra stopped smacking her cakes.

"Shh," Hades commanded.

Blood rushed to Than's face. He didn't like calling attention to himself, but he had to stand up for Therese.

Everyone waited silently for the Hydra to continue eating. She could be agreeable at times, but when frightened, she was vicious and terrifying. Although the group could likely contain her, they would all rather avoid fighting her if they could.

*It's true,* Athena prayed, once the sounds of cake-eating resumed. *Poseidon has been obligated to work against Therese in the past, but I've heard him speak fondly of her as he once did of Pelops.*

At that moment, Than felt their plan to bind Zeus had taken a turn for the worse. Although Artemis had previously mentioned attempting to gain Poseidon's alliance, this was the first plan to do so. Than believed Poseidon had too much invested in his partnership with Ares and Zeus and would likely report any suspicions of a rebellion directly to them. Poseidon might even imprison Apollo and Therese in his golden net and hand them over to Mount Olympus.

*I don't like it,* Than prayed. *We should move forward as planned, without Poseidon. We still have hope of converting Demeter to our cause.*

*Don't count on it,* Persephone said with a frown.

Than knew he was pulling at straws, but he had to say something.

*What do you think, Therese?* Artemis asked. *Would you be willing to go with Apollo to get a sense of Poseidon's loyalties?*

*I don't know how I can help,* Therese replied. *But of course I'm willing to go and try.*

Therese avoided Than's eyes. He couldn't believe it. Not again.

## CHAPTER TWO

# Earth Shaker and Dream Maker

Therese followed Apollo to the stables where he bridled two of his flaming red horses, Lampos and Acteon, to his chariot. As she stroked Stormy's mane in the stall beside Swift and Sure, she wondered how she could possibly add anything valuable to this mission. Artemis's comment was the first Therese had ever heard of Poseidon's supposed fondness for her. She shuddered at the memory of the earthquake two years ago at the Durango natatorium after she had refused Poseidon's help during her swim meet. He may have been kind to her before that moment—allowing her to ride his favorite dolphin, Arion—but his kindness had ended the year she had undertaken the five challenges of Hades. Poseidon had also tricked her during her quest for Artemis to replace Callisto with another bear in the sky. Worst of all, he had taken Athena prisoner, keeping her in a humiliating tube under the sea as though she weren't the venerable goddess of wisdom that she was. How did anyone expect Therese to help Apollo win over Poseidon's good graces?

Sitting beside Apollo in his golden chariot as they entered the Upperworld gave Therese the opportunity to study the god of light. With the exception of the events of last autumn during the attack on Athena and the Underworld, she hadn't spent much time with him, and never had Apollo and she been alone. It was true what everyone said about him: he was the most beautiful god, though she had a particular preference for Thanatos. She knew little about the golden god—aside from his powers of healing, prophecy, lie-detecting, and making music on his lyre. Those were things everyone knew. She wondered, as she glanced his way once more, what he thought of her.

"I know what you are going to ask me," he said suddenly.

"Oh?"

"You are going to ask me about my past with Poseidon."

Heat rushed to Therese's face, for that *was* what she was about to ask, though she had been thinking of other things. Without looking at Apollo, she squeaked, "And?"

"You've heard the story of how Poseidon and I built the Wall of Troy?"

"Um, sort of." She held on to the side of the chariot as they swooped down a mountainside toward the sea. "I read about it in school. Something about Hera's scheme to bind Zeus?"

"Yes," Apollo replied. "As you have come to learn for yourself, Zeus's libido has often led him astray from Hera."

Therese didn't comment, though she wanted to say plenty. The admiration she once felt for Zeus had faded these past few months.

"It's hard to blame Hera for attempting to outwit him," Apollo continued.

The chariot swerved past a headland and then skated across the Aegean Sea. Despite her anxiety over their mission, Therese took pleasure in the chariot ride. It was even more thrilling than flying, in her opinion.

"We might have succeeded in chaining Zeus if Thetis hadn't sent her one-hundred-handed monster to wake Zeus from his drug-induced sleep. Zeus grabbed his thunderbolt, and we were at his mercy."

"I read that he hung Hera up in the sky," Therese said, stifling a smile. The idea of the queen of the gods dangling, helpless, among the stars was pretty hilarious, given the queen's mean treatment of Therese over the golden apples.

"For one *day*," Apollo said. "She wept so loudly, he let her down."

Therese had a hard time imagining Hera weeping. She never showed her weakness, at least not that Therese had seen.

"Poseidon and I had a much longer punishment," Apollo went on. "For one *year*, we labored for a stingy, unjust king. He promised us payment if we could build a wall around his city in a single year, but he never expected us to do it. He didn't know who we were, and he treated us worse than slaves."

"Poseidon was against the Trojans in the war, then, right?" Therese asked.

"Right."

"But why did he make so much trouble for Odysseus, who also fought *against* the Trojans?" If Therese hadn't managed to contact Odysseus last fall when she and Than, Galin, and Cubie were trapped in Ida's cave…she shuddered just to think what might have happened.

"Because Odysseus made Poseidon angry. You don't want to get on Poseidon's bad side, if you can avoid it."

Therese was fairly certain she had already done that.

The chariot plunged into the ocean. Therese, now used to breathing underwater, enjoyed this part of the journey, too, in spite of the growing apprehension she felt over having to meet with the god of the sea. Before long, Arion and his pod were swimming alongside them, struggling to keep up with the flaming horses' electric speed. Therese gave her dolphin friend a wave, which he acknowledged with a nod. Then the palace came into view, its translucent crystal revealing the merfolk bustling around the foyer. As the chariot approached, the palace doors lifted open, and a trio of merfolk greeted them and unbridled the horses. Therese and Apollo were given a boulder each to carry to keep them from floating, and then they were led through a series of corridors to Poseidon's chambers, the walls of which were inlaid with Mother of Pearl.

Poseidon sat on his throne with his wife, Amphitrite, beside him. Two sea nymphs stood nearby.

"To what do I owe this unexpected visit?" the god of the sea asked.

Therese had no answer as she sat clutching the strap of her quiver, but Apollo was quick with his reply.

"Our newest goddess was asking me about the days we built the Trojan wall. I thought it might be fun to tell her our stories together."

Poseidon's face brightened, much to Therese's surprise. "Indeed, it would. Please have a seat, and I'll have my servants bring us some refreshments."

***

Jen held onto the rail of the catamaran beside Hip and shouted, "Woo-hoo!" into the wind. "Can you make us go faster?" Her dreams had never been so fun, and she was determined to make them fun for Hip, too.

"Of course," Hip said, laughing.

The boat sped up.

"Now take us Peter-Pan style, up into the night sky," Jen said.

"If you say so."

The boat lifted up from the sea and ascended toward the moon waning in a cloudy night. The sky was beautiful and the breeze exhilarating. The city below twinkled it lights up at them, as if it was enjoying the show above.

"Awesome!" she squealed as she looked around in amazement. "Have you ever done *this* before?"

"You can try all you like to come up with something new, but I'm telling you, you can't. I've done everything imaginable in the Dreamworld."

She frowned. "Well, that's no fun for you." She couldn't imagine a more boring life than to have nothing new to look forward to, and she was disappointed that every idea she came up with had already been thought of before by someone else. She had rather hoped she could be someone different for this magnificently beautiful god who, for whatever reason, had chosen to spend time with her.

Hip took her hand, lifted it, and twirled her around, as if they were dancing. When she spun around to face him, he smiled at her and said, "Watching you experience things for the first time…now, that's priceless."

He couldn't have said a nicer thing. She sighed and smiled up at him with delight.

He touched his lips to hers, and she closed her eyes and kissed him back, unable to believe that this beautiful god, who had done everything and had been everywhere, could be so wrapped up in her. How long would it last?

The gray clouds hid the moon, and for a while, they were in darkness.

"Why are you frowning?" Hip asked. "I could have sworn you gave me a brilliant smile only seconds ago. Do I kiss that badly?"

"You can see me?"

He laughed. "You seem to forget who you're talking to."

So gods can see in the dark. Every day, she learned something new.

"Therese told me what she had to do to become a goddess," she said.

"What did she say?"

"She told me about how she first had to avenge the murder of her parents. She couldn't do it. And then about the five challenges your father gave her. She couldn't do them, either."

"Did she tell you she could have been killed at any point, since the moment she decided she wanted to be like us?"

"Um." No, in fact, she hadn't.

"Even after Demeter's ritual, she could have been captured—was captured, in fact…"

"She told me about the Amazonian pit and that Norwegian dude…"

"What Norwegian dude?"

Jen clamped her mouth shut. Hip didn't know about the Norwegian dude? "Never mind." Why was he so angry? "Hip, what's going on?"

The moon appeared from behind the gray clouds, and she could see the worry on his face.

"I know what you're getting at," he said. "I don't want you to go there."

She took a step back. "You don't think I can do it? You don't think I'm as strong as Therese? Oh. Em. Gee! I'm a million times stronger than her—at least I was before she became a goddess."

Hip laughed, which made her angrier.

"It's not that," he said.

"Then what?" As soon as she had asked, she regretted it. What if his answer was that he didn't want to be with her forever? Her stomach balled into a knot. He hadn't even said he loved her, and she was already planning eternity with him. She looked away. "I want to wake up now. I have things to do."

***

"What a lucky break," Than whispered merrily to himself as he tucked Therese's flute, still in its case, beneath his arm and headed to his father's chariot. He flew to Mount Olympus with a tune on his lips, and after being admitted by the Seasons, found Apollo's lyre just where the god of healing had said it would be.

Zeus saw Than as he was about to leave Apollo's rooms.

"Well, now, Thanatos. What brings you to Mount Olympus? You're two days early for your engagement party."

Than had hoped to avoid the lord of the gods, though he knew it would be unlikely. He forced a smile and said, "Apollo asked me to get his lyre. He and Therese want to play together."

"And I wasn't invited?" Hermes asked, appearing from the dining room.

"Don't be offended, cousin. I'm sure they would have asked you had they known you were interested." Than wished it was another time when there was no tension between them, and he could invite his cousin with ease to join the concert playing.

"They can't know of it if they don't ask," Hermes said with a frown.

"There, there," Zeus intervened. "You'll have your chance to play with them at the party, Hermes. Right now, I have work for you to do."

"Sorry, Hermes," Than said, inwardly relieved. "I'll see you both soon."

Aphrodite entered the hall just as Than was leaving. Her face flushed when she saw him, and his wasn't long in doing the same.

"Aphrodite, I…" Than began, but struggled to find the right words. He missed his favorite aunt and hated how she ignored him.

"Good day, Thanatos." She had no smile for him. She gathered her skirts and shuffled past him, a few of her Graces following.

At least she had acknowledged him, which was more than she'd done lately.

As Than drove his father's chariot from Mount Olympus to the Aegean Sea, he prayed to Aphrodite, as he had done countless times. *Why do you still snub me, after all I've told you?*

He received no reply.

He tried to recall a time when there was perfect harmony among the gods, and he supposed there never was one, but rarely had their conflicts involved him. Although for centuries he'd been rebuked by the Olympians, he'd come to enjoy their respect and friendship in recent years. Therese had pulled him into their fold. He had become especially close to Hermes and to Aphrodite. For centuries the goddess of love had snubbed him, but only lately did it sting.

Swift and Sure dived into the sea, and soon he was greeted by a menagerie of merfolk and led to Poseidon's chambers. As he entered, he was glad to hear laughter. This was a good sign.

Than was surprised to find Amphitrite among them. The few times he had visited Poseidon's palace, she had not been at home, preferring to spend her time among the creatures of the sea. But here she was beside her husband with a goblet of wine in her hand and a smile on her beautiful face. She looked younger than Poseidon, though he knew her to be much older. Her long, sun-bleached hair was twisted up in an elaborate style, fastened with a golden net and a headband made of crab pincers. The pincers met and held one another at the center of her forehead, just above her turquoise eyes, which were the same shade as Poseidon's eyes.

"Welcome, Thanatos," Amphitrite said as Than entered. "As much as I've enjoyed hearing about my husband's good old days with Apollo, I'm eager for our concert to begin."

With a boulder in the crook of his arm, Than crossed the room to give the flute case and lyre to Therese and Apollo, who sat in ornate chairs close to and facing their hosts with a golden tray between them full of food and wine. Therese had a lovely glint in her eyes that made Than want to kiss her and that made him jealous of what he'd been missing.

"Why don't you stay, as long as you're here?" Poseidon offered.

Than hoped his face didn't betray his shock. Never had the god of the sea invited him to stay. A seat appeared beside Therese.

"Thank you," Than said, still unused to being accepted and welcomed by the Olympians. Having Therese in his life had made everything better.

Therese gave Than a smile as she assembled her flute. *We still haven't asked him anything about Athena.*

*These things take time*, he replied silently.

"You begin," Apollo said to Therese. "Play whatever you want, and I'll follow."

Than watched as Therese put her flute to her lips, closed her eyes, and played the first song she had ever played for him. He was whisked away by the music to those first days he was in her company, when she had unwittingly begged him to kiss her. The corners of his mouth shot up and he fought not to laugh.

*I'm surprised this works underwater,* she prayed to him.

Than winked. *Water is a better conductor of sound waves than air.*

"Oh, I love Handel," Apollo said with a feminine wiggle. "And this particular sonata is one of my favorites." He took up his lyre and harmonized with Therese's flute.

Than could not deny the beauty of the music reverberating through the room. If it were possible to weep underwater, he would. Poseidon and Amphitrite appeared equally moved. Maybe this wasn't such a bad idea.

***

Hypnos stood at a loss, unsure whether he should go, as Jen had asked, or force her to tell him what was wrong. It hurt him to see her so upset. He realized only recently how much of his happiness had come to depend on hers.

"I'll go, but not like this," he said to her back. He reached out and twirled her ponytail before dropping his hand to his side. "I hate to see the girl I love looking so sad."

She turned to face him. "You love me?"

The surprise on her face alarmed him. Hadn't he already made that clear? He supposed mortals needed to be told directly. "I thought you knew that."

"Then why don't you want me to be like you?" Tears filled her eyes and dripped down her cheeks.

He stepped closer and brushed her tears with his thumbs as he held her face. "You're safer as a mortal, Jen. I can take better care of you."

"But gods can't die," she said.

"There are worse things than death." The memory of the birds eating out his liver made him shudder.

"But I'll grow old, and you won't. I know that sounds vain and ridiculous but think about it. How will you still love me when I'm a wrinkled old woman and you're still young and beautiful?"

He had wondered the same thing, but, if he was honest with himself, he was less worried about *her* getting old as a mortal than he was about their *love* getting old as gods. Hadn't he ardently loved Pasithea, only to find his love grow cold in a matter of months? As much as he loved Jen right now, he was afraid he didn't have it in him to love one person forever. He hoped he was wrong.

"Hip? Are you listening to me?"

"Yes. And I'm thinking about what you're saying. You think about it too. We don't have to decide anything right now. It's not like lightning will strike us down if we don't decide your fate today."

"Oh, I almost forgot!" Jen said, as she dried her eyes. "I've been so wrapped up in myself, I forgot to tell you something important."

"I'm listening." He was relieved she was no longer cross. He put his arms around her waist.

"Pete's been trying to get Therese to come home on account of something my dad's ghost told him."

"I know."

"Well, yesterday Pete told me he prayed to Zeus about it."

"What?" Getting Zeus involved was not the best idea.

"Zeus asked Pete to give him the message, promising to pass it on to Therese."

"And so did Pete do it?"

"Not at first. He told Zeus the same thing he's told all of us. He wanted to tell her himself. But then a thunderstorm came over our house, and lightning struck a tree by our barn. Pete said then a god named Hermes appeared and demanded to know what my dad's ghost had said."

"Did Pete tell him?" Please say no, Hip thought.

Jen nodded.

"And what was it?"

"Pete refused to tell me, but he said it ain't good."

CHAPTER THREE

# The Engagement Party

Just as the music from Apollo and Therese came to an end, an urgent message from Hip made Than forget to applaud.

*Come home as soon as possible,* Hip prayed. *We need to talk.*

Apparently, Apollo and Therese heard the same prayer, for they exchanged worried looks in spite of the praises from Poseidon and his wife.

"Is something amiss?" Poseidon asked.

"My brother has asked us to come home," Than replied.

"He calls Apollo, too?" Amphitrite asked with surprise. "Why would Hypnos need the god of truth?"

"I do not know," Apollo said, since Hip had revealed nothing in his prayer. "But perhaps we should go and find out."

"It was a nice visit while it lasted," Poseidon said. "Thank you for coming."

"Thank you for having us," Therese said meekly.

Still seated in his chair, Apollo asked, "Before we leave, I have a sensitive question for you, uncle."

Than's body tensed. He wondered what Apollo would ask.

"Ah," Poseidon said with a stiff smile. "The true reason for your visit."

"One of many," Apollo said. "I did enjoy our trip down memory lane. That is not a lie."

"As did I," Poseidon said.

"But I also came to ask you about your feelings for Athena. Do you blame her for what happened a few months ago?"

"Blame her? I don't blame her for wishing to reunite with her mother, but I do blame her for threatening our king." Poseidon's face turned red.

"If there were a way to release Metis from Zeus's body without harming him, would you oppose it?"

Than held his breath.

"What of his wisdom?" Poseidon asked. "Some believe Metis is the source of it."

*How can Poseidon speak of Zeus's wisdom after that failed attack last fall?* Therese prayed to Than.

"If that's true," Apollo said, "Don't the rest of us gods have wisdom enough to counsel him when needed?"

"He's the mightiest of the gods," Poseidon said. "I don't think it's good for the mightiest to be the least wise."

"Not the least," Thanatos said. "But maybe not the most, either."

"The rest of us can balance out his might," Apollo said. "If it were ever necessary to do so, I mean to say."

"I can't imagine how such a scheme—of freeing Metis—could play out without there being dire consequences for those involved," Poseidon said.

"You can't imagine it because it offends you?" Apollo asked.

Than sat very still. No one could lie before Apollo.

"Metis is my sister," Amphitrite said. "I would like to see her freed."

"I have an open mind," Poseidon finally said.

Hypnos's urgent prayer came once more.

"We better take our leave." Than stood. "My brother calls."

***

Therese had not been in the Underworld long when she left with Hip in his father's chariot for Colorado to learn what Pete had told Hermes.

When Hades had warned them against god-travel, Than had wanted to drive with her, but Hip had convinced his brother to let him go instead. He worried Than's close proximity to the Holts would put their mortal lives in danger. Therese had agreed.

Hip waited, invisible in the snowy sky, while Therese appeared to Jen in the Holt family room. Therese did not reveal herself to the others. She put her finger to her lips and beckoned Jen from the sofa where she sat beside Bobby and across from Mrs. Holt watching TV. The family scene brought back so many memories from Therese's childhood. Sometimes she really wished she could go back to those days before her parents died, but then one look from Than would remind her how happy she was to be with him. As Therese and Jen climbed the stairs to the second floor, the familiar sound of Pete's guitar carried from the first bedroom. Therese entered without knocking and showed herself to Pete. Jen followed.

"We need to talk," Therese said.

Pete stopped strumming and lifted his face to her with his mouth hanging open, reminding Therese of how he looked when he was a golden retriever.

"It's about time," he said. "Sit down."

She looked around. Jen fell onto the bean bag in the corner, leaving the papasan chair for Therese.

"I need to know what you told Hermes," Therese said as she sat on the edge of the chair.

"He scared the hell out of me," Pete said. "If only you would have let me tell you earlier."

Therese took a deep breath, telling herself to be patient, but it didn't work. "Well, you can tell me now. Spit it out."

All her life, Pete had seemed so much older, bigger, and stronger. She had looked up to him for as long as she could remember. But today he seemed…fragile.

"I cut my finger and dropped my blood in a cup in the barn and called to my father's ghost," Pete explained. "My father came to me. His memory was hazy, and I wasn't always sure he knew me. It was like talking to someone with Alzheimer's, until he drank the blood."

"So what happened?" Jen asked.

"I asked him what would become of Mom. I wanted to know if I should stay living here, or if I was free to go off to pursue my own dreams."

While Pete had been pierced with Cupid's arrow, he had wanted to stay close to Therese and work on his parents' place. But once she had successfully neutralized the arrow, his old dreams of going on tour with his band seemed to resurface.

"And?" Therese asked, dreading the answer.

"His white eyes started rolling around in their sockets, and he said a whole bunch of stuff I couldn't understand. He said the number seven a lot, and he said moons and suns, and all kinds of mumbo jumbo, but the part I could remember is the part about you. He said the day you marry Death, the lord of Mount Olympus will fall, and someone close to you will die."

"Someone close to you or to me?" Therese asked.

"You." Then he added, "That's why you can't marry Than. I've been trying to tell you. I know you probably think I'm just jealous, but I'm not. Well, maybe I am a little."

"Pete…" Jen started.

"Look." Pete squared himself to Therese. "You can live with him, but you can't marry him."

Therese gawked, momentarily paralyzed. With this information, Zeus would no doubt do everything in his power to keep her and Than apart. Threats to his kingdom in the past had led to horrible consequences. It was why he swallowed Athena's mother. Would he swallow Therese, too? The Olympians already considered Than and her to be oath breakers, so Zeus would never take their word for it if they swore to never marry.

"I've got to get out of here!" Without saying goodbye to the Holts, Therese opened a window and flew to Hip where he'd been waiting in the sky. "Take me home!"

"To your aunt and uncle's?"

"No. To the Underworld." She took the reins from him and drove the chariot home.

That night she stayed in the safety of the Underworld rather than travel the world helping humans and their animal companions. Although Than was with her, he was also in countless other places, and she feared he was vulnerable to attack. Zeus couldn't afford to capture Thanatos, the god of death, could he? She supposed the king of the sky could return Hermes to the Underworld. Nervously sucking her bottom lip, she sat beside Than on their new couch between the two leather chairs facing the fireplace and begged him to be vigilant. She didn't want to distract him, so she tried not to talk much, but he reminded her that he could do billions of tasks simultaneously.

"There's really only one thing that distracts me," he said with a mischievous smile.

"Then stop thinking about it," she said seriously. "I don't know why Zeus hasn't already acted. It must be the party. He's waiting to capture us when we're on Mount Olympus."

The next day, wearing a dress of pale pink silk made for her by Ariadne, Therese followed Than down the winding corridor to his father's chariot, where most of the gods of the Underworld prepared to journey to Mount Olympus for the engagement party. Anyone watching from the outside would have thought they were attending a funeral, Therese thought as she reached the group and met their solemn faces. Even Alecto, who usually wore a tough exterior, looked anxious. As Therese climbed into the chariot beside Than, she tried to appear confident and brave, but she was far from both. Something was bound to go wrong at the party.

Than had said the night before, when they had discussed with the others what to do, that there was nowhere they could go to escape Zeus. It was better to face him and to be surrounded by allies than to run away and be alone and vulnerable.

She clutched the straps of her quiver and bow, which went everywhere she went.

After their journey, Hades, Persephone, Hecate, Hypnos, Tizzie, and Alecto waited on the rainbow steps, where music poured from the palace, for Therese and Thanatos to enter the hall first, since they were the guests of honor; but there was another reason: the other gods of the Underworld drew wards of good fortune with their swords on the gold-paved walkway around the palace before entering themselves. Therese's blood pumped madly through her veins. She put on a smile as she and Than moved to the center of the gods and bowed before Zeus and Hera, who were perched on their double throne at the far end of the room.

*I will not let go of your hand for the entire party,* Than reassured her.

All of the Olympians were seated at their thrones in the great ring around the room, but other chairs made of precious stones and metals had been brought in and were arranged both between and in front of the Olympians. Because these chairs were not on raised platforms, the other gods seated around the hall did not block the view of the Olympians, nor did those who were standing. Dozens of golden trays spread with food and drink added to the crowded room.

*Do not eat or drink anything,* Than told her again. *Stay busy talking, singing, laughing, but do not eat or drink.*

*I won't if you won't.*

*But don't be obvious about it.*

They had already discussed this, and it irked her that Than felt the need to remind her, as though she were a child, but she resisted the urge to say, "I know!" Instead, she smiled and continued greeting the other gods.

Therese and Than turned about the room to bow at each of the Olympians and the various lesser gods stationed near them. To Hera's left sat Ares with his sons, Phobos, Deimos, Anteros, and Cupid, at his feet. She marveled once more at how Ares and his twins shared the same color of red hair as she. A wave of panic overcame her, and she shot a look at Deimos, who only grinned.

She turned to Hermes and his son, Hermaphroditos. They sat with three satyrs Therese had never met. Asterion and Ariadne seemed to know them. They stood between them and Poseidon, who was joined by Amphitrite and two sea nymphs. The nymphs were presently distracted by the music being made by Apollo and four Muses. Apollo played his lyre, and the Muses sang in harmony.

*It really is beautiful,* Therese prayed to both Than and Apollo.

*Try not to look so frightened,* Apollo replied.

Therese was surprised to see Algaea, the oldest of Aphrodite's Graces, whom she knew to be Hephaestus's real and secret wife, seated beside him, along with their four daughters. They were beautiful, like the other gods, with light brown curls that matched their eyes. Therese had never met them but recognized them from Aphrodite's descriptions.

Next in the circle sat Hades and Persephone, in a double throne that had only recently appeared near the entrance to the hall. Hecate, Hip, Alecto, and Tizzie joined them. Meg had remained behind to defend the Underworld from another possible attack and to maintain Tartarus.

*So far so good,* Hecate prayed, the white streaks of her hair in sharp contrast with her black satin dress.

Therese gave her a weak smile.

There were two empty chairs among the other gods of the Underworld, which Therese supposed were meant for her and Than, but before being seated, she and Than continued to make their bows around the room.

The blood rushed to her face when Aphrodite and her Graces refused to acknowledge them. Even Pasithea, who once joined them for a game of night Frisbee, ignored them. Therese fought back the tears pricking her eyes. They were mostly tears of anger. Aphrodite was being unreasonable, and Therese was dying to tell her out loud to her face that enough was enough. But this was the first time Therese had been among so many gods and goddesses, and she wasn't about to show signs of weakness. Despite her anger, her heart was hurt by the snub. She loved Aphrodite best of all the gods outside of the Underworld.

Although the smiles on the faces of Artemis and Callisto and their fellow huntress companions did not make up for Aphrodite's treatment of her, they did bring a smile to Therese's face. Callisto had continued to express gratitude to Therese for rescuing her from the sky and reuniting her with Artemis. Therese's smile soon faded, however, when she noticed, for the first time since entering the room, Demeter's throne was empty.

Hestia said softly, "Demeter stays at her winter cabin during this time of the year and makes very few exceptions."

"I'm sure she'll be at the wedding," Hera added with a suspicious smile.

Therese bowed to Hestia and her entourage of maidens before finally locking eyes with Athena.

*Have you noticed anything unusual?* Therese asked the goddess of wisdom.

*I've unraveled nothing,* Athena replied. *If my father has a plan for tonight, I have no knowledge of it. Be safe.*

*I pray to you to help us.*

*I promise to do what I can to protect you,* Athena assured her.

Zeus's voice began over Athena's last prayer. "Now that you have had an opportunity to greet the guests of honor, I have an important announcement to make that I'm sure will thrill our couple."

Apollo and the Muses stopped making music, and the hall became silent. Therese squeezed Than's hand.

*What's going on?* she asked him.

Before Than could reply, Zeus said, "It is with great pleasure that I invite all of you here present today to a special wedding ceremony uniting these two love birds. Although I once mentioned the possibility of holding a wedding here on Mount Olympus, I have decided that Therese's mortal family and friends should not be denied."

*What?* Therese glanced at Than and saw her concern mirrored in his eyes.

"Excuse me, brother," Poseidon interrupted. "Are you suggesting that all of us here today should go down to earth and attend a wedding among mortals?"

"That's precisely what I'm—not suggesting, but commanding. It will be my gift to the bride and groom. After all, I can't imagine anything that would make the bride happier than to see both sides of her extended family in one magnificent wedding."

Hera stood beside her husband. "And it *will* be magnificent."

As the goddess of marriage, Hera was called upon to oversee the nuptial vows, and it was said that a bride and groom with her blessing would never part. Therese doubted she and Than would receive such a blessing after the prophecy Pete shared with Hermes.

The gods and goddesses applauded. Someone tossed glittery confetti into the air above them, and it slowly drifted, like diamonds, onto the crowd, making everyone sparkle. Therese forced a smile but wanted to explode with rage.

*We'll have to abort,* she prayed to Athena, Artemis, Apollo, and to the gods of the Underworld. *We can't put the lives of so many mortals in jeopardy.* There was no way she could allow Athena and the others to carry out their plan on her wedding day—not when the lives of the people she loved the most in the world would be put in harm's way. She glanced at Athena and could tell that her smile, too, was forced.

When the applause died down, Poseidon stood up and cleared his throat. "Am I the only god who sees the danger in having all of us on earth in mortal form at the same time? I fear some of us should remain behind to keep the world from crumbling, and I, for one, volunteer."

"Some of the lesser gods will remain behind," Zeus said. "But my gift to the couple diminishes in grandeur for each Olympian who does not attend. Now, if you ask me, brother, you're just trying to get out of having to wear a suit."

Zeus chuckled, but Poseidon frowned.

Zeus added, "And those legs of yours could benefit from an activity other than swimming. You look now as though you might topple over. Or is that because of the wine?" Zeus laughed more boisterously than before, and Ares and his children dared to join him.

Poseidon glared at Zeus but said no more as he returned to his throne.

*Someone else object!* Therese pleaded.

Hades stood, "Your gift is generous, but unnecessary, Lord Zeus. Therese and Thanatos appreciate the thought, I'm sure, but the splendor of your beautiful palace cannot be surpassed anywhere on earth."

Therese held her breath as she silently thanked Hades.

"Flattery will get you nowhere," Zeus said. "My mind is made up. I want to meet her mortal family."

Hades returned to his throne.

Zeus lifted his golden goblet. "We shall hold the ceremony in exactly six months, on the summer solstice."

Six months? Therese met Than's eyes. She didn't know how to feel about that. On the one hand, she was anxious to be Than's wife. The summer sounded so far away right now. On the other hand, it gave her allies time to regroup and plan their next move.

"We will hold the ceremony in Therese's beloved Colorado forest," Zeus continued. "Her parents will be able to watch from their special Elm tree. Won't that be splendid?"

Therese thought how nice it actually would have been, had the biggest scheme in the history of time not been wrapped up in her wedding plans. The gravel pad outside her childhood home was spacious and flat and would serve as the perfect place for folding white chairs. If the audience faced away from the house, they would see the reservoir to their right and the mountains to their left, and a huge line of pines as a backdrop before them. The deck that wrapped around the house would be a nice place for the reception. At least a dozen round tables and chairs could fit around it, not to mention the enclosed porch and the gravel path, which could be cleared after the ceremony to make more room for tables, if needed. Oh, it would have been perfect if Zeus had not been told that his fall would occur on that day. She bit her lip and sighed.

Zeus continued. "So let's raise our glasses to Therese and Thanatos and wish them a happy engagement as we celebrate their love with them today. Let there be joy, laughter, and music!"

The music began again. Than bowed to Zeus and led Therese across the hall to their seats by the other gods of the Underworld. Therese glanced at Aphrodite and managed to make brief eye contact with her before the goddess turned away. Therese slumped in her chair. At least for the moment, it seemed she and Than were safe.

A figure looming over her brought her from her reverie.

It was Poseidon. *I will stand with you and Athena.*

Therese looked up at him in shock. Was it a trick? His turquoise eyes were filled with rage. Could the god of the sea be trusted?

## CHAPTER FOUR

# Athena's Plot to Bind Zeus

The Parthenon was quiet after dark, when all signs of tourists and travelers were gone, and the gods, invisible to all but one another, stood in a ring to discuss their plan to betray their king. Unlike the Hydra's lair beneath Larissa Hill, where they dared not speak their plans out loud, in this refuge, they spoke, because Athena's wards around the Parthenon were too powerful for even Zeus to break. More importantly, there was no Hydra. Than had asked why they didn't always meet here, and the goddess of wisdom had said they must vary their meeting places so as not to arouse suspicion. She had reserved the Parthenon for the most important, and most dangerous, meeting of all.

"I can't go in my true form to the wedding," Than pointed out. He hadn't seen this move by Zeus coming. He felt blind-sided and a little hopeless. "I'd put all those mortal lives in danger."

"And I'd put them to sleep," Hip added. "So I can't go in my true form either."

"No, you cannot," Athena agreed.

"Which means," Than could hardly say it. Their plans were crushed in one move. Check mate.

"We'll no longer have our greatest power at our disposal," Hip answered for him. "And it was crucial to our plan. The power of disintegration."

Therese put a hand on Than's arm. He covered it with his own and hoped she did not already regret joining him in this dangerous life.

"I understand…" Athena started.

"I don't think you do," Than said. "This means some other god outside of this circle will likely be assigned my duties. And that means…" A cold sweat came over him, and he shuddered.

"I'll make sure the person who replaces you is one of our own," Hades declared. "I am the lord of the Underworld, and no one shall tell me how to rule my kingdom."

"Hermes can't be trusted," Than said, though it pained him to say it.

"I'll find someone who can," Hades assured him.

"I understand your concerns," Athena said to Than and to the other gods of the Underworld, who had been as fervent as he and Therese in arguing for a delay in their plan to bind Zeus.

His parents, his sisters, his brother, and Hecate had all pleaded his case.

"The problem is," Apollo said again, "I can see our success at the *wedding*. I cannot guarantee our success if we wait for another occasion."

"What about my family and friends?" Therese asked Apollo. "Can you see if they get hurt? Pete said someone close to me will die."

Than wanted to go back in time and change the course of the future. Zeus was hitting him where it most hurt: Therese's family and friends. She would be devastated, and so would Than.

"I only see us with Zeus," Apollo replied. "I'm sorry, Therese. I can't see beyond that."

"Listen to me," Athena said, looking directly at Than. "I know this would be hard on you and your bride. I'm sorry that Zeus has thrown this wrench into our plan. But our choices are either to give up completely on this mission, or to follow through on the day of your wedding. We have no other alternatives."

Than started to object, but Persephone spoke first. "Ariadne could be convinced to meet with Dionysus on another day."

Persephone referred to a deal they had made with the god of the vine. If he helped them to overpower Zeus, Ariadne would agree to meet with him the day of the wedding.

"Hera will be most distracted during the vows," Hephaestus said. "We have to keep that in mind."

"And don't forget Nemesis," Artemis added. "She agreed to balance out the fortune between Therese and Zeus during the nuptials. I can't go back and ask her to alter her plan. It was hard enough to get her consent in the first place."

"But we don't need her," Hades said. "As much as I admire her for doling out justice, now that we have Poseidon on board, neither Dionysus nor Nemesis is necessary."

Than was still not sure they could count on Poseidon.

"But let's not dismiss their contributions," Artemis said.

"We need all the help we can get," Hephaestus agreed.

Athena's face reddened. "Can we trust Poseidon?" She turned to Apollo.

"I need an opportunity to interrogate him," Apollo said. "He made his vow to Therese, and I wasn't privy to it." Then he added, "Even so, as I've said again and again, I can only see our success at the *wedding*. I can't see it anywhere else."

Hades tugged his dark curly beard and said, "We must weigh the benefits with the costs. Is the risk of losing an innocent life worth our chance to save Metis, who has already been a prisoner in Zeus's body for centuries? Is it right to expect a mortal to pay this price?"

Than noticed the eyes of the two Furies present—Meg and Tizzie—turn red with blood, and he felt a beacon of hope rise in his chest. Perhaps his father's moral point about the costs and benefits would move the rest of the gods to see the wrongness of their plan, but the beacon was squashed when Therese's face took on a look that was all too familiar to him. He groaned.

"This isn't *just* about saving Metis," she said. "This is also about saving Cybele, and maybe even Melinoe. This is about standing up for women who have been bullied by Zeus for too long."

"You would sacrifice a loved one?" Persephone asked.

"I've come to accept that there are worse things than death," Therese replied—and Than could see the vein at her neck pumping fiercely. "Zeus cannot be allowed to wrong others. We need a more just king." She looked across the room at Hades. "If Apollo can see our success, we must go forward."

The corners of Athena's mouth lifted, and her gray eyes gleamed.

Than recognized what this meant. It wouldn't matter how much he objected. If Therese was willing, the mission was a go. The problem was, although Apollo could see them successfully bind Zeus, he could not see beyond that. Than had a feeling none of this would end well.

***

As the gods departed the Parthenon, each with his or her instructions from Athena, Hypnos chastised himself for not speaking up during the meeting. A part of him wanted to keep secret the strong feelings he was developing for Jen. If Ares got wind of them, the god of war might assume Jen would attempt to follow in her friend's footsteps toward immortality, and another deity in the Underworld would only further threaten him. Hip did not want Jen to be any more involved with the gods and their drama than she already was. But on the other hand, Pete's prophecy unsettled him. What if the person close to Therese fated to die at the wedding was Jen? Would he be able to bear the sight of his brother guiding her will-less soul to the Underworld, never to be held in his arms again?

He decided to speak with his brother privately about the matter.

He waited a few hours, until Therese had gone with Apollo to visit Poseidon. Although Than was in thousands of places, he was also pacing nervously before the hearth when Hip approached Than's room. Hip could sense him on the other side of the door.

"Hey, bro', can I come in?" Hip asked.

The door opened. "Of course. Is something wrong?"

What *wasn't* wrong? Hip neither said the question aloud nor prayed it. He crossed the room in one big leap and landed on a leather chair before the fireplace. "You got any wine?"

Hip glanced around at the addition of Therese's things in the room as Than poured wine into a goblet and handed it to him. She had moved in with Hecate for a while but had recently moved back in with Than.

"Thanks. Aren't you going to have some?"

"I'm not thirsty."

Hip chuckled. Than really was the practical one of the two of them. In Hip's opinion, thirst was seldom a requirement for drinking wine. He took a sip and then asked, "You and Therese holding up?"

"As well as we can. I think she's preparing for the worst."

"She still upset with me for telling Pete how seers summon ghosts? I warned him not to do it. I told him what would happen to him."

Than shrugged, but that was enough of an answer.

"I suppose the Fates are punishing me for that," Hip said.

"You?" Than stood up, suddenly angry. "How is any of this a punishment for you? Therese stands to lose at least one of her loved ones. There could be countless others. Just because Mr. Holt's ghost didn't see others doesn't mean there won't be."

Hip regretted coming. It was obvious to him that Than had no idea how much he had come to love Jen Holt. Hip hadn't meant to upset his brother. "You're right, bro'. I'm sorry." He stood to leave.

"Wait." Than slapped a hand on Hip's shoulder, locking him in place. "I'm the one who's sorry. Sit back down and tell me why you came to see me."

***

The others had already turned out their horses and had gone inside, but Jen needed to ride. Bobby had been anxious to get cleaned up for his date in town, and Jen's mom hadn't been feeling well, so the two of them had cut out early. Only Pete had remained, riding Ace behind Jen and Sassy for another round or two along the fence line. But now, he was gone, too, and it was only Jen and Sassy beneath the setting sun in the cold, cold dusk trotting through the already trampled blanket of snow beneath them.

She needed to get the god of sleep out of her head, but she couldn't stop seeing his charming smile and broad shoulders and deep blue eyes and… Turning from the fence line, she steered Sassy up the hill toward the stream, where some of the horses were gathered beneath the lean-to. She wished she could un-love as quickly and as hard as she had loved.

Why did he have to be a god?

If he were a normal boy, she'd have a decent shot, but a god? The thought of being his plaything for a year or two, or however long it would be before he got bored with her, made her stomach churn. She pulled up to the stream, brought Sassy to a stop, and dismounted just in time to be sick. As she wiped her mouth with the back of her glove, she let the tears fall.

But not for long.

She refused to be pathetic. She bent over and grabbed a handful of snow before smearing it over her closed, swollen eyes. She did not want to be this heart-broken, love-sick girl who could not control her emotions. At nineteen, she had plenty of time to meet someone new, but that would never happen as long as she continued to call Hip. She had to move on. It was the only way to protect herself from further pain.

And yet, she had come to realize, as she'd gotten older, why her relationships with real boys never lasted. She was afraid of getting too close. It was her father's fault. Therese had told her to get counselling, but then Jen would have to talk about it.

A shiver moved down her body. In some ways, Hip had been the perfect boyfriend—always just out of her reach. But the day he tired of her would hurt like hell.

She climbed back on Sassy and rode to the pen. Before she reached it, she heard a strange sound coming from inside the barn. After dismounting, she cautiously led the mare toward the barn. The last thing she wanted was to come face to face with her father's ghost. She couldn't see it like Pete could, but that didn't mean it wasn't there.

"Pete?" she called before entering.

"They see you!" he cried back.

She dropped Sassy's reins and stepped inside. Pete was standing with his eyes closed, his palms turned upward, and his head nodding—not slowly, but like a man riding fast down a bumpy road.

"Pete?"

"They see you, Jen! Dad says watch out. You could be their key!"

"What are you talking about? Let's go to the house! You're scaring me!"

Pete's head continued to nod, even more frantically than before. He looked like a lunatic. "They think you may be their key!"

"Whose key? What are you saying?"

"The gods!"

Jen grabbed Pete's arm, but he could not be pulled from where he stood. He opened his eyes, suddenly, causing her to shriek.

"Jen?" His voice was back to normal, and he was no longer nodding. She still held his one arm, but the other had dropped to his side. "What do you want?"

She trembled uncontrollably. "Let's go back to the house. Please."

***

When Therese entered her living quarters, Hip was sitting across from Than in conversation. They looked up at her as she crossed the threshold.

"How did it go with Poseidon?" Than asked.

Therese removed her quiver and bow and laid them on a table before crossing over to the new couch between the leather chairs. She nestled her back in one corner, kicked off her boots, and stretched her legs across the cushions. Clifford came from his bed in the next room and jumped onto her lap. As she stroked his fur, she said, "Apollo couldn't get a clear reading."

"What does that mean?" Hip asked.

"It means Poseidon isn't sure himself where his loyalties lie," Therese replied. "It means Poseidon hasn't made up his mind."

They were silent for a while as Therese kissed the top of Clifford's head and continued to stroke his fur. She felt optimistic about Poseidon. Despite his flaring temper and past alliances with Ares and Zeus, Therese had a special fondness for the god of the sea that began in her childhood with her love of the water. Suspicious that the boys might be communicating without her, she scrutinized their faces and noticed that Hip looked less jovial than usual, and, on closer inspection, sad.

"So, what's up, Hip?" she asked nonchalantly.

He gave a look that said, *Really? You have to ask?*

It was Than who spoke next. "He's worried about Jen."

Therese's mouth went dry. Of course, he'd be worried for Jen.

"I'm sorry," she said. "I'm worried, too."

Jen was, after all, her very best friend.

She would never admit this to anyone—she could hardly admit it to herself—but she hoped beyond hope that the person fated to die on her wedding day was neither Jen nor Lynn. It wasn't that she hoped it was Carol or Richard or any of the Holts or her other friends. None of them deserved to die, and any one of their deaths would be agonizingly painful. And she hated herself for playing this morbid game of favorites in her mind. But she wanted her best friend and her little sister to have a chance at a longer life.

Therese had thought about going to the Fates and asking them to tell her the outcome, but she was too afraid of their answer. She'd already learned once that nothing good ever came from knowing the future.

*Two, but none immortal.*

"Have you heard who's been assigned your duties yet?" Therese asked the boys.

"Mortals can go without good sleep for the ceremony," Hip said. "But Hecate is slated for Death."

Therese nodded. That was the best choice, but she was disappointed that her friend and ally would not be by her side on the best and worst day of her life.

She let out a deep breath and sighed. "Well, Than, are we ready to head to my aunt and uncle's for Christmas?"

Than turned to Hip. "You sure you can handle my duties for two days on top of your other concerns?"

Hip stood up and offered his fist for a bump. As Than reached his knuckles to Hip's, the god of sleep said, "I told you, I got this, bro'. Plus, you said you'd relieve me every so often. Right?"

"Right."

Therese watched as Hip faded from their sight. Despite his upbeat demeanor, he could not hide his frown.

"He's in love with her," Than said, once Hip was gone.

"Oh, no."

CHAPTER FIVE

# Christmas in Colorado

Lynn played patty cake with Therese as Carol pulled up the calendar on her ereader, the lights from the Christmas tree behind her reflecting on the screen. "But the summer solstice is on a Sunday. You sure you don't want to have the wedding on the twentieth?"

Therese glanced over at Than, who said, "My family is a bit eccentric."

*That's putting it mildly,* Therese prayed to Than.

Than grinned, obviously trying not to laugh. "They, uh, they have their hearts set on the twenty-first. Is that okay with you?"

"I don't have a problem with a Sunday wedding," Richard said. "And you want to have it here, you say? That's nice. Really nice."

Therese was relieved that Richard wasn't overwhelmed by the idea.

"Yes, sir. And my uncle would like to preside," Than said.

"He's a pastor?" Carol asked.

"Um," Than turned his worried eyes to Therese.

She hadn't really thought of anything to explain. She fought the blush that was threatening to sweep across her face, and then an idea hit her.

"A judge," Therese said. "Is that okay?"

Carol and Richard glanced at one another before Carol said, "We aren't particularly religious, so that's fine with us, isn't it Richard?"

"I'm fine with it," he replied.

Therese let out a heavy breath.

Lynn climbed from Therese's lap and ran across the living room to her toy box. Clifford followed, and with a little bark, distracted Therese from her worries by telling her he wanted a new toy of his own. He snagged a plastic dinosaur and happily set to chewing on it. Lynn didn't seem to mind.

Jen, who sat on the other side of Therese on the sofa from Than, said, "How many, um, *people* are we talking about?"

Therese shot Jen a look that said, *Watch it.* She knew Jen was going to slip up and say something about the gods.

"I have a pretty big family," Than said.

"How big?" Carol asked.

"Oh, let's see," Than appeared to be doing math in the air.

Therese calculated: twelve Olympians plus their spouses and partners made twenty-four or so. Most of them had at least three children, so thirty-six more, if they all came. There were also attendants. She wondered who Than was including.

"Okay, so that makes…seventy-one. Hold on." He turned to Therese. "Do you think Phobos and Deimos will come?"

"Yes, unfortunately," Therese replied.

"Then seventy-three."

Carol paled.

"Did you say Fear and Panic?" Richard asked with a look of surprise.

"Huh?" Therese asked her uncle. What did he know of the twins?

"Phobos and Deimos," Richard repeated. "Fear and Panic, the twin sons of Ares."

"W-wait a second," Jen stammered. "You *know* them?"

Therese shot another look of warning in Jen's direction. She just knew Jen was going to blow it for them.

"Know them. Of course. I love Greek mythology. It's what led me to my love of reading, and eventually to my degree in journalism. So you have relatives named for the Greeks?"

"His family *is* Greek," Therese explained, full of relief once more.

"That's right," Than said.

"But Than doesn't sound Greek," Richard said.

Than said, "It's short for…"

"Than-cu-leez," Therese interrupted. If Richard knew what Phobos and Deimos meant, then he'd recognize Thanatos, too.

Jen giggled.

*Thancules? Really?* Than prayed. *Are you sure you want to go with that?*

"How unusual," Carol said.

*You want to tell them the truth?* Therese asked Than.

*But Thancules? Why not Thantiope or Thancleod?*

*What's wrong with Thancules?*

Than rolled his eyes. *You know how I feel about Hercules.*

Oh, yeah. She'd forgotten that he thought of the demigod as all brawn and no brain.

"So seventy-three for your side of the family," Richard said. "That's quite a few. But don't worry. We can handle it."

Carol looked less sure.

That's when Therese realized her aunt and uncle were worried about the cost. "Oh, I forgot to tell you. Than's parents are loaded, and they insist on paying for the whole thing."

"What?" Carol couldn't suppress her smile as she glanced at Richard. "We can't let them do that."

"Of course, you can," Therese said.

"They won't have it any other way," Than added.

"We aren't poor church mice," Richard said. "We can help. Plus, we have a few folks we'd like to invite as well. Nanna and Paw-Paw and Uncle Joe will want to fly up from San Antonio."

"No!" Therese said. The fewer mortals at her wedding the better. "I mean, that's not necessary."

Richard looked hurt. "They would be devastated if we didn't invite them."

"Of course, we should invite them," Carol said.

"Of course," Therese agreed. "But if they can't fly up, it's okay."

"Of course, they can fly up," Richard said. "Don't you want my parents and brother to come?"

"I, I, yes! Oh, Richard, yes!" Oh, shoot! Therese hadn't meant to hurt her uncle. She was trying to do the opposite.

"You don't think an outdoor wedding in summer will be too hot for the humans?" Jen asked.

Everyone looked at Jen, perplexed, except for Therese, who wanted to pinch her.

"I, I mean, as opposed to the animals," Jen recovered quickly. "Clifford won't mind the heat, but what about the rest of us?"

Therese inwardly groaned but had to admit it was a decent recovery. That Jen!

"I'm sure it will be fine," Richard said.

"If this was Texas, I'd be worried," Carol added. "But Colorado is still pretty nice in June, especially up here in the mountains."

"It's the afternoon rain we need to worry about," Richard said. "We should play it safe and have the ceremony early, like around eleven. We could serve a lunch afterward."

As they discussed more of the details of the wedding—Richard talked about getting fans and misters, if necessary—Therese relaxed a bit.

Than gave Therese a conspiratorial wink, which made her smile.

"And you have to invite Todd and Ray and their families," Jen put in.

Therese frowned as the anxiety swooped down on her again. "I wasn't really planning on it."

"What?" Carol shot up from her chair. "Therese? Is there something bothering you? Something I need to know?"

"Huh?" Therese didn't know what to say.

Carol looked back and forth between Than and Therese. "Why don't you want any of your friends and family to come? Is there something you're not telling us? Are you, I mean…" Carol's face turned red as a tomato. She glanced over at Lynn, who knelt near her toy box. Then Carol lowered her voice and asked, "Are you pregnant?"

Hot blood rushed to Therese's face.

"Maybe you two should go upstairs and talk," Richard, whose chocolate complexion had also turned red, said to Carol.

"No," Therese managed to say. "I'm not pregnant. There's nothing wrong. I just, it's just that Than's family is so big, and I never really wanted a big wedding."

"A big fat Greek wedding," Jen said, laughing.

Carol returned to her chair. "Sorry. I…" her voice trailed off.

*That was awkward,* Therese prayed to Than.

He looked like he was about to burst out laughing.

Lynn ran across the room with a huge plush toy. It was a brown dog with floppy ears. She hurled it onto Than's lap and said, "My doggie."

Clifford looked from his half-chewed dinosaur and gave a little bark that meant, "What am I? Chopped liver?"

*What are you doing to that toy?* Therese asked him, glad for the distraction.

He bent down his head and tail, turned his back to her, and then returned to his chewing.

"I like him," Than said of the big plush toy.

"It's a girl!" Lynn corrected.

"Oh, I see. What's her name?" Than asked.

"Terry!"

Therese smiled as tears flooded her eyes. She inwardly laughed at herself. All this talk of mortals coming and putting themselves in danger and of pregnancy, and her tears were brought on, not by those things, but by her little sister naming her toy dog after her. "Aw. You named your doggie after me?"

Lynn nodded her cute little pig-tailed head.

Therese glanced at Than. *If anything happens to her, I'll never forgive myself.*

*I have an idea*, he replied.

***

Than disintegrated and went to see his grandmother at her winter cabin near the base of Mount Kronos. She called to him before he had reached her door. In fact, he was still miles away when she spoke to him. He often forgot how powerful she was, but why should he? She was the sister of the greatest Olympian gods. Why wouldn't she be powerful, too?

"Come inside, Thanatos," she said.

He found her seated at her table with her head in her hands. She might be powerful, but just now she appeared totally incapacitated. How could such a supreme being look such a mess? When she lifted her face to meet his eyes, it was red and pinched-looking, her eyes swollen and flooded with tears.

He sat across from her. "Do you weep like this all winter?"

She sighed. "It's my affliction, but it's also my friend. I can't let the sadness go after all these years."

He'd never felt sorrier for her, had never seen her in such despair. Why did she come to this lonely cabin in the woods when she could be with him and the rest of their family all autumn and winter?

"You should come and live with us in the Underworld. It's not such a bad place."

"What brings you way out here, Thanatos?"

So she would change the subject. He cocked his head to one side. "Have you heard that Therese and I are to be married on the summer solstice?"

"No. Congratulations." She gave him the hint of a smile. "I'm glad I'll be on Mount Olympus to see it."

"It won't be at Mount Olympus," Than said. "It will be in Colorado, at Therese's childhood home."

He went on to explain Zeus's announcement, but he did not reveal Athena's plan or his suspicions of Zeus's counterattack. Instead, he said, "There's been a prophecy that someone close to Therese will die on our wedding day. We want you to come and sit with her little sister and protect her from harm."

"If the girl is fated to die, there's nothing I can do…"

"We don't know the identity of the person referred to in the prophecy," Than said. "And we don't know which choices we make affect future outcomes. Your hand in this may be the reason only one is mentioned in the prophecy and not more."

Demeter eyed him up and down. "You make a good argument. I suppose I can do my best to protect the child."

Than stood up and smiled, full of relief. He was glad to have something positive to tell Therese for once. Demeter's protection would bring his bride great comfort. "Thank you," he said.

***

Later that night, Therese pretended to get ready for bed—though neither she nor Than would be sleeping. He was down in the basement on the sleeper-sofa, which Carol had made up with fresh linens. Therese and Than planned to leave once everyone else was asleep. Than would relieve Hip, so Hip could return to his duties, and Therese would take Hades's chariot—parked a little way up the mountain behind her house—to answer as many prayers as she could during the seven or eight hours before morning.

As she waited for Carol to come in and wish her a good night, she snuggled with Clifford on her old bed, just like they used to do. A rush of nostalgia came over her as she recalled those days when she was still a little girl, and her parents weren't birds and could hold her in their arms, and there was nothing at all to worry about. Although it was winter and cold outside, she had opened her window so her parents could sit on the sill and talk to her. She and Clifford were immune to the cold, and though Therese spoke with her parents nearly every day through prayer, it was nice to see them and to speak with them out loud. When they spoke, they made the most beautiful bird sounds, but Therese could understand them just as she could the speech of all animals. She hadn't told them about the prophecy, or Athena's plan, or the counterattack they were expecting from Zeus, because she didn't want to worry them. Consequently, when they spoke to her, they were full of excitement.

"There's a big white plastic container in the attic," her mother said. "It has my wedding gown in it. You don't have to wear it if you don't like it, but I just wanted you to know it was there, in case you *would* like to wear it," her mother chirped.

Therese climbed from the bed and crossed to the window. "Oh, Mom! Why didn't you ever tell me about it before?"

"You were only fifteen when we died," her father said.

"But still…" Therese argued.

"Actually, I did once, when you were really little. I think you were five. I dressed you up in it and took photos of you. I thought I put them in one of the albums."

"I've never seen them," Therese said.

She sensed Carol coming up the stairs, so she kissed her parents good night, closed the window, and returned to her bed.

Carol knocked before entering. "It's freezing in here! Did you have the window open?"

It was difficult for Therese to sense just how cold it was.

"I needed a little air."

"Should I get you another blanket?"

"No, thanks. I'm fine."

Carol sat on the edge of the bed and hugged herself to keep from shivering. "I'm sorry for what I said earlier. I should have known better."

Therese was thankful for her aunt's apology. She had hoped Carol wouldn't pretend she had never said anything. The accusation stung.

"That's okay. Don't worry. I know I've been acting kind of strange."

"Are you having second thoughts?"

Therese sat up. "No. Not at all. I promise." She hoped she wasn't giving anyone that impression, especially Than. Therese had never felt surer about anything in her life.

"Just…"

"I love Than. He's the sweetest, most thoughtful, most trustworthy person on the planet. I admire him so much, more than any boy I've ever met. I wish you could have the chance to get to know him better. I'm telling you, he's the one for me."

*Aren't you laying it on a little thick?* A prayer from Hypnos came unexpectedly.

*Hip? Quit spying on me!*

*I'm on my way to see Jen.*

"Just because you know he's the one doesn't mean you have to rush into anything. Richard and I waited a few years, and I think it helped us make a stronger beginning."

"I've known Than for almost four years, Carol. I know not all girls are ready this young, but I am. I really am."

"What about college? Are you planning to finish those online courses?"

Therese twisted the covers in her hands. She had nearly completed her degree in psychology, but there was no way she could tell her aunt. She would think it impossible. And it was impossible for a normal girl. "Yes. I may even finish early."

"Is it still psychology?"

Therese nodded. "It will help me get a job as an animal caretaker and trainer."

Like Apollo and some of the other gods, Therese hoped to integrate into the company of humans as often as possible. With a degree, she could even get a real job, which she hoped would make it possible for her to help more people and their animal friends. Plus, the psychology had already come in handy more than a few times.

"Are you still working at the animal shelter?"

"Yep. I love it."

Carol smiled. "I guess it's a good thing Than's parents are loaded."

Therese laughed. "You don't need to worry about us. We'll be fine."

Carol nodded—her body more relaxed—and said, "I have an idea, but tell me what you really think, not what you want me to hear, okay?"

"Okay."

"What do you think about having Lynn as your flower girl?" Carol's eyes were gleaming, but Therese's heart was breaking. "I know she won't be quite three by the wedding, and she might do something silly, but even if she messes up, she'll still be adorable. We could give her a basket of rose petals, and she could…"

"Carol, stop," Therese said, feeling the blood leave her face. As much as she would love to see Lynn in a pretty dress carrying a basket of flower petals, all she could see was how much more danger her little sister would be in if she walked down the aisle alone among all those gods.

The gleam left Carol's eyes, and she blushed. Even her ears turned red, nearly the same color as her hair. "I'm sorry. This is your wedding."

"No, I'm sorry." Therese felt terrible. She could see she had taken some of the joy away from her aunt.

Tears formed in Carol's eyes. "It was a silly idea. She'd steal the attention away from you, where it should be."

"I, I just want to keep things simple." She knew she was breaking her aunt's heart. Tears flooded her own eyes, but she refused to let them fall. "I'm sorry."

"That's okay." Carol patted Therese's knee and gave her a big smile. "It's no big deal. I'm just happy for you."

Carol stood up and then bent over and kissed Therese on the forehead. "I love you, sweetie. We'll talk more in the morning."

"I love you, too."

"Lights off?"

"Sure."

"Merry Christmas Eve Eve."

"Merry Christmas Eve Eve."

As soon as Carol left and closed the door, Therese hugged Clifford.

Clifford licked a tear from her cheek. "She doesn't understand," he barked.

"I know, boy," Therese said. She wiped her eyes on the bed sheet. "Come on. We better get going. I'm looking forward to driving the chariot tonight. That will cheer me up."

She opened the bedroom window, where her parents were still perched, looking in on her.

"It'll be okay, Sweet Pea," her father chirped.

Her mom asked, "What doesn't Carol understand? I thought having Lynn as a flower girl was a lovely idea."

"She wants to keep it simple," her father said.

"I better go," Therese said, evading the conversation. "I hear a dog trapped in a tar pit in Oklahoma City. I'll see you two later."

Hades had urged Therese to take his chariot instead of Stormy in the event Zeus decided to act before her wedding day, so, with Clifford following behind, she ran up the mountain where Swift and Sure were waiting.

"Hey, boys," she said to the horses. "Thanks for waiting for me. Are you ready to go?"

They neighed an affirmative.

With her sadness over the wedding plans replaced by total excitement, she climbed into the chariot beside Clifford, took the reins, and launched into the bright night.

There was something thrilling about riding in a chariot, especially this one. Apollo's and Poseidon's each had their perks—Apollo's was pulled by beautiful flaming horses and Poseidon's could move like lightning underwater—but only Hades's chariot had the ability to cut into the narrowest of passageways and turn on a dime in any direction. As frightening as her life had become among the gods, zipping through the sky behind Swift and Sure reminded her how much she loved it.

***

When Hip finally arrived in mortal form to visit Jen in her bedroom that night, the first thing he said was, "I can't stay long."

Enough already. She was tired of never spending real time with him.

"What? Why not?" Jen asked.

"I've been covering for Than, and now I have to return to my own duties," he explained. "But I wanted to drop by in between to snatch a kiss from you in person. They taste so much better this way."

He leaned over where she lay and touched his mouth to hers.

She had to admit the kiss was exquisite. A soft, involuntary moan escaped her throat.

He squeezed her shoulders and looked at her longingly. "You make me so happy," he said.

She felt the same way but didn't say it. Even though they rarely met outside of her dreams, every minute with him was worth the long wait.

He kissed her again. His flesh against her flesh was warm, and his breath smelled like musk. She pushed her fingers through his hair and held onto him. Maybe he could be the one to help her get over her issues. As he leaned closer and allowed the weight of his upper body to lie against her, she heard him groan. Her grip moved from his hair to his shoulders. He felt so good. She could barely breathe, but she didn't care.

"I have to go," he said, though he remained on top of her.

She was partly relieved, though she wanted him to stay. She said nothing as he stood, blew her a kiss, and disappeared.

***

The next morning, Than followed Therese's instructions in making sure he looked as though he had been sleeping all night. He mussed up his hair, put on a pair of pajamas Therese had bought specifically for this purpose, and twisted up the bed covers. It was actually kind of fun. Never in his ancient life had he needed to play act. Well, that wasn't true. He supposed he had to play act when he first came to the Upperworld to try and win Therese's heart. But this was different. He waited until the others were awake and moving around, until the smell of fried eggs and potatoes and coffee wafted down the stairs, before he headed up to greet them.

"Merry Christmas Eve!" Carol called from the kitchen.

"Thanks," he said. "Merry Christmas Eve." He was a little familiar with the various traditions around the world celebrated during the winter solstice, and Christmas was no exception. For centuries, people in the Northern Hemisphere had created ways to make the darkest season brighter and cheerier with wreaths and trees of lights. Before electricity, they used candles. In recent history, Than could see whole blocks of houses alight with strings of electric-powered lights as he flew across the night sky to retrieve the souls. He learned over the years that people were especially heart-broken to lose a loved one during their holiday season, a time spent celebrating peace on earth and goodwill toward one another, a time when families spent days together and were thankful for their blessings.

Richard stood beside Carol in the kitchen turning the eggs. He asked Than how he liked his cooked.

"Oh, any way is fine with me," Than said. He had no idea how he liked them cooked. Eggs, for the most part, were not a common food item for him.

"Did you sleep okay?" Carol asked, handing him a mug of coffee. "Sugar, right?"

Than smiled. "Right. And I slept fine, thanks. Where's Therese?"

Lynn slapped her hands against the tray of her highchair. "Terry! Where Terry?"

Than had a brief thought of what it would be like to have a daughter with Therese.

*Two, but none immortal.*

"She's already eaten," Richard said. "She's up in the attic, looking for something."

*What are you doing in the attic?* Than asked Therese.

*Don't come up! It's a surprise!*

Richard handed Than a plate of eggs and fried potatoes. "Here you go, son."

"Thanks."

Carol gave him a fork and napkin and put shakers of salt and pepper in front of him. "How would you feel about driving into town with me today, Than?"

"How would I feel about it?" He wasn't sure what Carol was asking him. He shoveled in the food and found it tasty. He'd forgotten it had been a long time since his last meal.

Carol sat on the barstool beside him and leaned her elbows on the granite countertop. "I want to get something special for Therese for Christmas, but I need your opinion. She's been gone so much these past two years. I hardly know what she likes anymore."

Richard gave Than a sympathetic look. "I doubt the boy wants to go shopping on Christmas Eve. The traffic will be a nightmare, and the crowds can get pretty ridiculous."

Than had never been shopping before in his life, though he'd fetched souls from mobs of shoppers over the years. Fighting the crowd for merchandise did not sound enjoyable.

"I have something in mind, though," Carol said. "I just want Than's opinion before I make the final purchase. One store. That's it. Please?"

Than could not deny his future mother-in-law. "Of course, Carol," Than said. "I'd be happy to go with you."

"Wonderful!" She squeezed his shoulders and seemed a little surprised by their girth. He hid a smirk as she recovered and added, "Then you can drive. I hate holiday traffic."

Than gave Carol a forced smile. *Did you hear that?* he asked Therese. *She wants me to drive.*

*Make sure she fastens her seat belt,* Therese replied. *Boy, is she in for the ride of her life!*

***

Therese admired herself in the dusty attic mirror. The scooped neckline and capped sleeves were simple yet elegant. The skirt was not too full, either, and reached to the floor. It might even need to be hemmed, Therese thought. She wished she could remember the time her mother dressed her up in it, but she could not and could only imagine how her mother must have pinned it in the back to keep it from slipping from her little shoulders. She sighed at her reflection now and couldn't believe she had gone all these years unaware that the dress was up here, waiting for her.

*You look beautiful,* her mother chirped from the little round window.

*I can still recall how your mother looked the day she wore that dress,* her father said. *Just as lovely as you.*

"And more," Therese said, though she had to admit that her own looks improved the day she became a goddess.

*Don't sell yourself short, kiddo,* her dad said.

Therese turned toward the window and her parents. "I wish you could give me away," she said to her father.

Her father didn't reply, and Therese fumbled with the beads on her bodice, regretting her words, sure she had only dampened everyone's mood.

*I can give you away,* he sang suddenly. *Ask Richard to do it, and I'll be sure to fly just above you. We'll both do the honors.*

The corners of Therese's mouth nearly reached her eyes. "Really? That would be so great! That would mean the world to me!"

Her nervous anxiety over the plot to bind Zeus was for the moment replaced by sheer thankfulness and gratitude for the gift of her parents and their involvement in her wedding. In the months after their deaths, she could not have imagined that her mother would be there to give her a wedding dress and her father to give her away. Tears pooled in her eyes as she went to the window and kissed the tiny beaks of her favorite cardinals.

***

Than rarely drove the orange Lamborghini. He had purchased it with Therese over a year ago in memory of their first driving lesson together with Hermes. As he ushered Carol outside and into it, the memory of that first driving lesson made him smile. He missed his cousin. It seemed he had just gotten to be good friends with the messenger god when the conflict broke out and spoiled their trust. He hoped one day they could rebuild that trust and enjoy one another's friendship again.

"This is one fancy car!" Carol said as he flipped open the doors.

"Thanks."

"Aren't you cold?" Carol asked from the passenger side as Than climbed behind the wheel. "You forgot your coat."

He felt a blush coming on. Unused to relating to mortals, he'd forgotten he needed to blend in. He and Therese had brought coats, but he had left his in the basement. He conjured a replacement coat in the backseat and grabbed it before laying it on the console between them. "I'll put it on when we get there. I don't like to wear it while I drive."

Luckily, it hadn't snowed since the day before yesterday, so the driveway didn't need shoveling. The sun shined in a cloudless sky and melted some of the white powder, which dripped from the branches of the evergreens surrounding the cabin and roadside. As Than pulled the car from the gravelly drive, the car slid and turned ninety degrees in the wrong direction.

"You probably aren't used to driving in the snow," Carol said, gripping her armrests. "I didn't think about that."

"Don't worry," he said, sounding more confident than he felt. "I'll get us there and back in one piece." He maneuvered the car back in the right direction and, after spinning the wheels, slowed down, gained traction, and headed onward.

Once Carol had guided him past the dam and off the country roads to the main road toward Durango, she told him about her gift for Therese.

"I had a locket made with a photo of her parents on one side and a photo of Richard and Lynn and me on the other," she explained. "It's even waterproof, so she can swim without taking it off, if she wants."

Than knew Therese would be pleased. "She'll cherish it," he said.

"I hope so. She's not easy to buy for anymore." Carol pointed ahead. "Mind that stop sign!"

Than slammed on the brakes, causing the car to fish tail for several feet before coming to a stop in the middle of the intersection.

"Sorry about that," he said. Luckily the only other car in sight was ahead of them.

Carol patted her chest with one hand, calming herself. "That's okay. I should have warned you it was coming."

He eased his foot onto the accelerator and continued toward town, trying not to get flustered by the prayers she unwittingly sent to him

*Please don't kill us, Than. What was I thinking asking you to drive?*

"The reason I asked you to come with me to the jewelry store is so you can help me decide how she would most like to wear the locket. I noticed she already wears one around her neck."

"My aunt, Athena, gave it to her."

Than knew better than anyone how much Therese treasured her locket. She never took it off, and he couldn't imagine ever looking at her without seeing the round, golden object hanging just above her heart.

"It's lovely," Carol said. "Therese showed it to me once. I've forgotten what it says."

"The most common way people give up their power is by believing they have none," Than recited.

"That's right," Carol said. "I like that. So inspirational."

"It's helped Therese," Than said. "It reminds her of her inner strength."

"Well, since she wears it around her neck, I thought I should give her something other than a necklace. Like maybe a bracelet or a ring. They make these really cute ring charms. What do you think?" Then she added, "You do see that truck ahead of us, don't you?"

Than eased on the brake pedal, and Carol sighed with relief.

"I think a bracelet or a ring would get in her way while she's doing her work," Than said, thinking specifically of the way Therese drew her bow and shot her arrows. A dangling locket at her wrist or on her hand could be cumbersome.

"You mean with the animals?" Carol asked.

"She uses her hands a lot. I'm afraid the locket wouldn't be easy to wear every day if she had to wear it on her wrist or finger."

"Oh, dear. Maybe this wasn't a good idea after all." Carol frowned. "Oh, turn left at the next light, but slow down a bit more, maybe."

"Her locket from my aunt reaches her breastbone," Than said as he yielded to oncoming traffic before making the left turn. "Why don't you have your locket fitted onto a shorter chain, so that it would sit higher, near her throat?"

"You don't think she would mind wearing two lockets?" Carol asked.

"She would love them both," he said, this time feeling as confident as he sounded.

"Turn into the next parking lot," Carol said. "You'll have to slow down if you don't want to donut."

When they reached the jewelry store, Carol took his hand and squeezed it. "I really like you, Than," she said. "I'm so glad you'll be a part of our family." Then she wrinkled her nose. "But, if it's okay with you, I'll drive us back home."

***

Jen opened the oven door, lifted the lid from the roasting pan, and checked the ham.

"It looks good, Mom," Jen said. "I think it's ready."

Her mother stood over the counter mashing sweet potatoes. "Did Therese say we would eat at six, or to arrive at six?" her mother asked.

"Eat at six. We should probably get there earlier. Like five, maybe."

"Will you be ready by then?" Bobby said from the sofa. "You haven't even showered."

"Don't you sass me, Bobby," Jen said. "Not from where you're sitting while I'm in here cooking."

"Now, now," Jen's mother said. "No fighting on Christmas Eve."

Pete entered the house from the barn and came into the kitchen to wash his hands. "Is Hip going to be there?" he asked Jen.

"I doubt it," she said, though she'd been hoping he would. She tried not to think about it, but deep down inside, she'd been wishing all week—ever since Therese's aunt and uncle invited the Holts to their Christmas Eve dinner.

"Are y'all into each other or something?" Bobby wanted to know.

"Bobby!" Jen's mother reprimanded. "That's none of your business." Then she turned to Jen. "Are y'all?"

"Mom!" Jen pulled the roaster from the oven and set it on the stove before turning the oven off. "I better go wash up."

As she skipped to the stairs, she heard Pete answer for her. "I think they are, but I'm not sure it's a good thing."

Later that evening, the four Holts piled into the Suburban with their arms filled with platters of food carefully covered in foil. Jen was proud of how tender her ham had turned out. As they approached Therese's driveway, though, her nerves fluttered beneath her skin.

*Please be there, Hip.*

Colorful strands of Christmas lights outlined the railing of the wrap-around porch, adding a festive flare to the occasion. Therese and her family greeted the Holts with hugs and "Merry Christmas Eve," as platters of food were handed over and carried to the kitchen. Jen scanned everyone's faces and accepted a hug from Than but frowned when she saw Hip wasn't among them.

*Of course he isn't here.*

Why had she allowed herself to think otherwise?

Warm cocoa, hot apple cider, and cold eggnog were passed around in mugs and glasses, and small plates of chips and dips and crackers and cheese were eaten as appetizers before the big meal. Carol and Richard carved the turkey in the kitchen as Lynn ran around with wrapped packages she kept digging out from beneath the tree. Jen's mom and Bobby were being entertained by the toddler, laughing at the funny things she said.

"Dis one's a wobot! Wight? A wobot!" Lynn sang happily, shaking a big wrapped box half her size.

"I think she means *robot*," Bobby said, laughing.

"Wat I said? Wobot!" Lynn assured him.

Pete and Than sat with Therese by the cozy fire, and Pete looked more relaxed for once, which was rare these days. He'd been spending way too much time in the barn saying strange words and bobbing his head up and down, like some kind of Native American shaman. Although Jen was disappointed that Hip had not come, she was surprised to find herself filled with joy and gratitude for the smiling friends and family surrounding her. A tear threatened to fall down her cheek, and it wasn't one of sadness. Even after all that had happened—her father's recent death, Pete's decent into lunacy, and her frightening induction into the world of gods by Melinoe the Malevolent—she was overcome with happiness by the sight of Christmas.

Therese brought Jen from her reverie by beckoning her over and patting the small space next to her in the recliner.

"We can both fit here," Therese said.

Jen smiled and squeezed onto the chair beside her friend and was glad when Therese wrapped an arm across her shoulders and caught her up with the conversation.

"Pete was just telling us about the new stallion," Therese said.

"We named him after the General," Jen said. "Did he tell you the General had to be put down?"

"Yeah," Therese said. "That's too bad."

"He was really old," Pete said. "He had a long life."

"Good for him," Than said.

Soon it was time to eat, and after, they exchanged gifts. Carol and Richard gave Jen's mother a beautiful quilt Carol had found at a craft store in Pagosa Springs. Squares of horses alternated with squares of pines and log cabins. Along the border were smaller squares alternating with guitars, boots, and cowboy hats. It was beautiful.

Jen's mom had brought loaves of her famous banana bread already wrapped in freezer paper so they could be eaten throughout the year. Everyone loved her mother's banana bread.

Lynn tore open a few of the presents from beneath the tree. She'd been right about the robot and had apparently picked it out at the store. For the rest of the evening, the conversation was punctuated by the beeping sounds and monotone words of the blinking, slow-moving robot.

Later, after slices of pumpkin pie had been eaten and dishes had been put away, after leftovers had been divided among them and thank-yous and good-byes had been shared, the Holts loaded up the Suburban with their food and gifts and headed home.

Jen helped her family put away the food and unload the gifts and then headed upstairs to her room. When she opened the door, she was shocked to find Hip, in mortal form, sitting on her bed with a gift in his hands.

CHAPTER SIX

# Artemis's Contest

One day in January, Therese responded to a distress call coming from a woman in Dorset, England, about her pet red fox, Anya. The woman explained that her sweet little fox had been bought from a special breeder in Russia for almost five thousand pounds and had become an important part of her family in the past three years. The woman and her husband had built an outdoor enclosure for their Anya that reached a full acre and was fenced along the ground as well as the sides, but their little digger had somehow managed to find her way out and had been lost for four days. Even though fox hunting had been outlawed, people in the countryside continued to practice it, since the law was difficult to enforce and since it was an important part of their family traditions. The woman prayed to any god who would listen to please help her to find her Anya before the hounds did.

By this time, Therese had stopped taking the chariot, against Hades's recommendation, because she refused to live in fear until the wedding, which was still a full five months away. Plus, it wasn't fair to Stormy to leave him idle in the Underworld stables. So she and Clifford mounted Stormy and sailed through the air to England in search of Anya, the red fox.

The woman, whose name was Belinda, prayed frantically. Therese wondered why she had waited four days to ask for help. In the two years she had been a goddess, Therese had discovered that it was typical for people to use prayer as a last resort when it should be the first thing they tried.

When the English Channel came into view, Therese descended, searching with her keen eyes for Belinda's home in the countryside. Stormy passed a ridge of bluffs, skirted down a deep limestone ridge, and headed into a low-lying valley full of trees and few country roads. There among the sparse cottages was Belinda's, and, sure enough, less than a mile away, a fox hunt was taking place with at least a dozen hounds and four horsemen.

Therese attempted to hone in on the foxes in the area, hoping to distinguish Anya from the wild ones. Meanwhile, she commanded the hounds, "Do not kill."

She watched with amusement as the pack of dogs circled in on one another, barking and whining.

"You've confused them," Clifford said.

"I know," she replied. "Poor things. I've asked them to go against their instincts."

"And their training," Clifford added.

Therese didn't normally interfere with hunts of this nature, but someone's animal companion was in danger, and it was her job to save it.

Amidst the horsemen and their confused swearing, Artemis appeared. The two goddesses spotted one another immediately.

"You've crossed the line into my territory," Artemis exclaimed. "I've ordered the hounds to continue their hunt."

"But there's a domesticated fox lost in these woods," Therese said. "I need to find her and return her safely to her humans."

"Foxes were never meant to be pets," the goddess of the hunt insisted. "People could use a good lesson."

"Artemis, please," Therese objected. "The woman is frantic. She's loved this fox for three years."

The hounds picked up the scent of a fox and ran through the woods, barking with excitement. The four horsemen shouted hurrahs and followed the pack. Therese took Stormy among them, commanding all foxes in the area to hide.

"You can't command the wild animals!" Artemis glowered at her. "How dare you!"

The wild animals would already know to hide. Therese had given the command for Anya's sake.

Artemis gave the foxes a counter-command.

Up ahead, through a dense wood, a red fox scrambled up a tree. Since most red foxes didn't know how to climb trees, Therese suspected this could be Anya. She called out to the fox by name, and the animal responded. The hounds picked up the scent and circled the tree, barking ferociously. Therese shot each one of them with her arrows of love until their barks became inconsolable whines. But by then, the horsemen had already spotted the fox.

To Therese's horror, Artemis jumped into the tree and flung the fox down into the pack of hounds. The hounds whined but did not attack. The horsemen swore.

Then Artemis took her bow and fitted an arrow to it.

"No!" Therese pleaded.

Artemis let the arrow fly. Therese god traveled from Stormy's back and took the arrow in her thigh. Fire seared through her flesh. She gritted her teeth, scooped up the fox, and god traveled back to Stormy.

"Where did it go?" one of the horsemen cried.

"One of the hounds must have it!" another said.

Artemis followed Therese. "This isn't over, goddess of animal companions."

Therese left the huntress and delivered the fox to the ground just outside its enclosure, where Belinda's husband knelt mending the hole in the fence. The fox poked its head up through the hole and was spotted by the man. He said Anya's name, and she leapt into his arms.

When the man called to his wife, Belinda ran from the house with glee. Therese was overjoyed by the reunion, but she knew Artemis had meant what she had said about this not being over.

***

Than was not happy. He looked across his sitting room at Therese, who leaned against the stone wall with her arms crossed. The wound from Artemis's arrow had already healed, but Than wished it had remained as a reminder to Therese of the danger she was in.

"The timing of this couldn't be worse," he said.

"We can't live our lives in constant fear," Therese said. "And this is important."

"Why can't this matter be settled in court?" Than grabbed the poker by the hearth and stoked the wood. He loved the smell of burning wood, and the flames it produced were less harsh than those cast by the Phelegethon.

"You know why."

He turned to face her again. "No, I don't. Taking this matter to court could be a welcomed diversion from all the tension between the Olympians. Working together to solve a common problem could help ease some of the tension." Plus, he didn't like her running about out in the open, unprotected. No one knew what Zeus's plans were, even if Apollo did see them all at the wedding.

"What would be the likely ruling?" Therese said, folding her arms more tightly against her chest. "The last time we asked the court to settle something, it ended in a contest, remember? Me against McAdams."

"I remember," he said bitterly. Why did she have to get so snarky when he only wanted to protect her?

"Artemis is going to kill Anya if I don't accept her challenge."

He moved across the room and put his hands on her shoulders. She was beautiful, even when angry. "You are the most compassionate person I know. I love that about you."

"But?"

"But this is one fox, and these are dangerous times."

"Than!" She huffed and pulled away from him, crossing the room toward the mantle. "When, since I've known you, have these not been dangerous times?"

She had a point. Never.

"Don't you think I have even the slightest chance of winning?" she asked, suddenly subdued.

He went to her and took her hands. "Of course, I do. I'm not worried about the outcome of the contest. It's how vulnerable you'll be during the contest that worries me."

"Apollo sees our wedding. Nothing's going to happen."

"He's not like the Fates, Therese. His visions change. What he sees is not set in stone."

She lowered her eyes, and he could tell her mind was hard at work, searching for an answer. It must have found it, for she looked up at him with a fierce expression on her face.

"If I win, I get to protect all domesticated wild animals, without her interference, *forever*. I can't back away from this challenge. It's not just about Anya. It's not just about you and me. This is about animal companions around the world for all of time. I have to try. Don't you see? It's my purpose."

He did see. His heart burned with love and admiration. The corners of his mouth twitched into a smile, but before he could say a word, she reached up and kissed him.

***

The African savanna—an immense, flat grassland with a few trees here and there—spread before Therese from where she stood in Kenya, on the edge of the Serengeti. A pride of lions took refuge in the shade beneath a tree about a mile away. A few miles further out were taller trees and a tower of giraffes. Therese sensed elephants in the woods between the giraffes and a swamp region, before the terrain returned to grassland. A herd of gazelle and another of zebras grazed in a region outside of Tanzania, which marked the finish line for this footrace designed by Artemis. Between there and where she stood was a cacophony of birds and insects.

Artemis came up behind her. "Ready?"

She looked up to see Helios, at high noon, above her. A few miles away, Athena hovered in the sky looking down at her. Therese and Artemis had each been allowed to choose a judge. She had chosen Athena. Artemis had chosen Apollo. He stood thirty feet in front of them with a red piece of cloth held high above his head.

"Ready," Therese said.

Apollo brought down the cloth, and Artemis soared past Therese. They tromped through the grassland toward the woods and the giraffes, but Therese was never able to make up the distance she lost from her late start. The ground quaked below their feet, and soon all of the animals were running across the savanna, too.

After treading through the muddy swamp and broaching more woods outside of Tanzania, a judge wasn't necessary to declare the winner. Artemis won by at least a mile.

But that was okay. The swimming race was next, and Therese felt confident she could win this one.

***

Jen sat on her bed gazing at Hip's gift with awe. She had been so surprised last month when he had presented it to her on Christmas Eve. It looked like a regular snow globe, but when you shook it and said the right words, images from the Dreamworld appeared in a burst of light and color and sound. It gave the person holding it the ability to see anyone's dreams simply by saying the name of the person whose sleeping mind he or she wished to invade, but Hip's main reason for giving it to Jen was for another reason: anytime, day or night, she could say his name and he would appear to her in the globe without putting her to sleep. He would not only be able to hear her, as he always did when she prayed to him, but now she would be able to hear him in return. They could communicate this way whenever she wished.

The rest of her house was quiet. Everyone else was already asleep, but now that she had the globe, she wasn't as anxious to sleep as she once was. She enjoyed watching him at work in the globe, and, since he was aware of her watching him, he usually added funny commentary. He was hilarious.

Just now he was walking beside a boy through a wide dungeon dimly lit by torches. She could see them from behind. Hip immediately sensed her, turned back to her, and winked. She covered her giggle, even though the dreaming boy couldn't hear her.

"Give me the dice, Dungeon Master," the boy said to Hip. "I need to see if I can open that door."

A huge wooden door loomed before them.

Hip said, "Dude, you don't need to roll. Just open it."

"The magi warned me that…" the boy stopped in his tracks.

"What?" Hip asked. He turned back to Jen, shrugged his shoulders, and turned his finger in a circle by his head to indicate the boy was crazy.

The door burst open. Both Hip and the boy jumped back and yelped in surprise.

A huge red dragon with shining scales and a horrible woman's face glared at them with bloodshot eyes. Hip had once explained to her that figments—which were eel-like nymphs—took the shape of beings from the dreamer's subconscious.

"It's my mother!" the boy screamed.

The boy turned and ran in the opposite direction of the dragon as a sharp forked tongue shot out from the dragon's mouth and whipped the boy.

"Do you get that symbolism?" Hip stopped to ask Jen. "This is about how his mother speaks to him."

The sharp tongue lashed out at the boy. Hip jumped up and snatched the dreamer, saying to Jen, "But you should see his room. It's a pigsty. No wonder she yells at him." Then to the boy, Hip said, "Don't run. Offer her a gift!"

The boy stopped. His arms and legs trembled in fright. "Give me the dice, Dungeon Master!" he cried.

"They are under your bed in your messy room," Hip replied. "Now give the dragon what you came here to give her!"

"No, Dungeon Master!"

Goblins appeared from the cracks in the walls and surrounded them on all sides. "Oh, hell," Hip whispered. "This kid is stubborn."

Jen giggled again.

Hip leapt from the dungeon and gave her a serious look. "Something's going on in your brother's dream."

"Bobby's?"

"No. Pete's. Come on."

The colors and lights shifted in the globe, and soon she could see Hip standing beside Pete and her father's ghost in their barn.

She shuddered at the site of her father's ghost, which she could see with clarity in the dream globe. Although it was transparent, it looked exactly as her father had appeared just before his death. A shiver rushed down her neck and spine, and a tight knot formed in her belly.

Pete was shaking all over, his head bobbing faster than ever, like he was being electrocuted from the inside.

"Help me!" Pete cried.

Jen stood from her bed, holding the globe with both hands. "What's happening to him?" she asked. "Can we wake him up?"

"I'm dangling from an iron chain. I don't know where!" Pete shrieked in a voice that sounded nothing like his. "Go to Melinoe, Hypnos! Make her show you where I am!"

"It's Cybele!" Hip said. "She's trying to contact me through your brother."

"Help him!" Jen screamed into the globe as Pete faltered to the ground in the fits of an epileptic seizure. She tried to remember that this was only a dream, but it seemed too real.

She dropped the globe on her bed and ran down the hall to her brother's room where he was seizing on his bed in the same way he was in his dream. She shook him fiercely, calling his name.

"Pete! Pete, wake up!"

***

In Alexandria, Egypt, where the Nile River emptied into the Mediterranean Sea, Therese stood beside Artemis full of the excitement she used to have before a meet. She bunched her hair beneath her swimmer's cap and pulled down the arms of her wet suit, noting the scoff of superiority from her competitor. Unlike Artemis, who wore her usual leather skirt and boots, Therese wore the gear, not for protection from the elements (which she didn't need), but for diminishing the friction of her body against the water. In this race against the northern-flowing Nile all the way to its southernmost banks in Rwanda, she would need every advantage she could take.

"No flippers?" she asked Artemis as she clamped hers to each foot.

"Don't need them," the goddess said with the smile of a victor.

Therese would not allow her opponent's confidence to unsettle her.

*I can do this*, she said to herself. *I have the advantage.* She had more than the wetsuit and gear; she had years of swim team experience on her side.

"Have you already chosen an archery course?' Therese asked, as they waited for their signal.

"Don't need to," Artemis said. "The contest ends in Rwanda."

If Therese were to lose this race, the contest *would* end, and she could no longer protect domesticated wild animals that inadvertently ended up in a hunt. But if she won, the contest would be settled by a final competition using their bows and arrows.

Athena hovered above the river about thirty yards high holding the same red cloth Apollo used on the African savanna. Apollo was already in Rwanda, waiting.

"Are you ready?" Athena asked.

Both goddesses cried, "Yes!"

The red cloth was lowered, and the two goddesses flung themselves into the river.

***

Hip disintegrated and dispatched to his father and mother to report to them what had happened in the Dreamworld.

"I think Cybele is trying to reach me through the seer," Hip said to them. "His sister woke him before I could get the full message."

Hip hated that the Holts were once again involved in the lives of the gods, but he couldn't withhold this important information that might be the key to saving Cybele.

"Can't you return him to the deep boon of sleep to hear the rest of it?" Hades asked.

"I could," Hip said. "But I thought it might be more fruitful to send an emissary to question him in the Upperworld. Messages can be garbled in the world of dreams."

"Good idea," his mother said. "But whom should we send?"

"Therese is the most logical choice," Hip said.

"Yes, but Apollo should go with her," Hades added. He turned to Hecate, who sat with her familiars on the other side of the room. "Go and ask Apollo and Therese to meet with me as soon as possible. This may be a way for us to finally save the manly goddess."

Hecate stood and disappeared at once.

Hip's heart filled with anxiety over the impact Cybele's use of Pete would have on him and his sister.

***

Than watched with pride as Therese's arrow found its target directly beside Artemis's. Three times they shot and three times they proved themselves to be equally matched.

"It's my turn to call the contest," Therese said with a confident smile. "You said I could call anything."

Artemis lifted her chin. "What will it be?"

"Music," Therese said.

"But I play no instrument," Artemis objected.

That was true, Than thought. Artemis shared none of the musical talents of her twin brother.

"You mentioned no restrictions," Therese said.

That was true as well, Than thought with a grin. Just when he thought he couldn't be more impressed with Therese, she goes and proves him wrong.

Athena's gray eyes gleamed, and she shared a smile with Than.

"What she says is true, sister," Apollo said.

Therese beamed with pride as she produced her flute and played. Artemis conceded the victory with a scowl. Domesticated wild animals everywhere howled a victory song for their goddess, and all of the gods heard it.

Hecate appeared before them. "Hades wants to see Apollo and Therese immediately."

The joy in Than's heart was now squelched with worry. What could his father want with his bride now?

<u>CHAPTER SEVEN</u>

# Pete and Cybele

Once again, Therese found herself seated beside the god of light on his golden chariot flying through the evening sky toward Colorado. He looked more solemn than usual, but she hesitated asking him why. After a few minutes of biting her lower lip, her curiosity got the better of her.

"Are you okay?"

Apollo looked at her with a gentle smile, which relieved the knot in her belly and helped her to relax.

"I miss someone. That's all."

"Do you want to talk about it?" she asked.

He drew his eyebrows together and sighed. "Becoming one of us almost cost you your life—many times. And even as a goddess, you've faced great peril."

She wondered how the topic had changed to her.

"But I want you to know something," he continued. "Most mortals who fall in love with a god end up settling for a lonely life. As you've discovered, we are all so busy that we cannot devote the time we should to the one we love. It breaks my heart to see someone pining away for me when there's little I can do about it."

Therese had no idea what to say to this, but her mind soon left the chariot and Apollo to focus on her best friend. Would Jen end up settling for a lonely life because of her feelings for Hip?

They were quiet for the rest of the ride as dusk settled over the countryside and Helios was no longer visible on the horizon. Soon the San Juan Mountains and Lemon Reservoir came into view. Apollo steered Lampos and Acteon to a landing in the forest near the top of the mountain nearest to the cabins, and, then together, he and Therese made their way down the trail toward the Holts' place.

As they neared the house, Therese could sense Jen and her brothers in the barn, but what drew her attention was the presence of Mr. Stern—Vicki's dad—visiting with Mrs. Holt at the kitchen table. She indicated to Apollo that she wanted to listen in on the conversation, so the two of them entered the house in invisibility mode to eavesdrop.

Mrs. Holt blew cigarette smoke from one corner of her mouth, away from Mr. Stern. Her gray hair had grown out from its usual bowl cut, and every few seconds, she brushed it out of her eyes with the same shaky hand holding the cigarette.

Mr. Stern looked less thin in his flannel shirt and fleece vest—robust, even. His brown hair was cut short and neatly combed to one side. His face was shaved, and his brown eyes, which had been perpetually shadowed with dark circles, gleamed brightly across the table from Mrs. Holt.

Mr. Stern said, "Maybe he's just restless. Maybe he needs to go out on his own for a while."

They were talking about Pete.

"I think it's more than that, John," Mrs. Holt said. "I've tried to get him to go with me to see a doctor, but he refuses. I'm worried he's losing his mind. That boy has been through a lot."

"It's tough for a kid to lose a parent."

Therese closed her eyes as the guilt and shame flooded through her. He was thinking of Vicki.

"That's not it," Mrs. Holt said. "Though I'm sure that was hard on all of 'em. You see, he feels guilty, because he's the one who reported his father to the police. I didn't even know what was going on under my own roof. Makes me feel like hell. And when Pete confronted me about it, I didn't believe him. He did a really hard thing getting his own father put behind bars without my support. I think the whole experience has done something to his mind."

"Maybe."

"Some people's minds just aren't as strong as others," she added. "I had an uncle lose his to schizophrenia. They say it runs in my family. That's why I want to get Pete looked at."

Poor Pete, Therese thought. She hadn't realized he appeared to be so bad off. She had to put a stop to his ghost visits before his behavior made his mother even sicker with worry.

Although Therese wanted to stay and listen to more of the conversation, Apollo motioned for her to follow him from the house to the barn.

***

Jen and her brothers had already turned the last horse out to pasture and straightened up the barn. There wasn't anything left to do, but she waited around, biding her time, wanting Bobby to go inside so she could have a word alone with Pete. Bobby had gotten obsessed with coiling a rope.

"I'll finish that for you," she offered.

"Nah,. I got it," he said. "You can go on in."

She fished around for something else to do. Pete was just standing there, in the corner, gazing at an empty stall.

"What are you doing?" she asked him.

"Waiting for you to leave," he replied.

"Why?" She looked across the barn at Bobby, but he kept his eyes on his rope.

"I want to talk to Bobby. Now go on inside."

Oh. So, they'd been waiting for *her* to leave.

"Why can't I hear?"

Bobby groaned. "Why did you have to tell her that? Now she ain't ever gonna leave."

"That's not fair," she objected. "Y'all leave me out of everything. You don't know what it's like being the only girl."

"Here we go," Bobby said.

"I've got something private to tell him," Pete said. "That's all."

"You talked to Daddy's ghost again, didn't you," she accused. "I told you to stop that. It's what's making you sick."

"You don't know that," Pete said.

"Yes, I do," Jen insisted. "It's the only explanation. You were fine until you started coming in here at night and drawing your own blood. You don't think I ain't noticed all those cuts on your arms?"

"It's the only way to call him," Pete said. "He's not in his right mind without the blood."

"He has no mind!" Jen shrieked. "He's dead. You've got to stop this!"

"Go on inside," Bobby interrupted. "I want to hear what Pete has to say."

Jen crossed her arms at her chest. "I ain't going anywhere. He can say it in front of me, too."

Just then, Pete fell to the ground, his body shaking like bacon in a frying pan.

Jen dropped to her knees beside him, wishing now she hadn't been so hard on him. He was more delicate than she realized. "Bobby, go get Mom!"

"What's happening to him?" Bobby asked.

Pete's eyes rolled to the back of his head so that only the whites were visible. His mouth strained open, his tongue swollen and slapping against his lips. He was trying to speak.

"Cy-Cybele," he stuttered. "Apollo, hear me."

"Just go, Bobby!" Jen hollered.

Bobby ran from the barn.

Jen shrank back when Therese and another god, beautiful and golden haired, appeared in the hay, on their knees beside her.

"Are you doing this to him?" she asked them.

Therese shook her head and put a finger to her lips.

What on earth was going on? What were these gods doing to her brother?

The golden god beside her, with golden brown hair and evergreen eyes, looked down at Pete and said, "Cybele?"

Pete's body shook more fiercely. His head jolted from side to side. Then, all at once, his body went limp.

"Pete!" She wanted the gods to go away and leave him alone, sure that they were the ones causing his affliction.

In a strange voice he said, "Melinoe may know where to find me. An impenetrable blindfold impedes my sight. I'm dangling by a chain at my waist, from what, I do not know."

"Oh, Cybele!" Therese cried. "Don't worry! We'll find you!"

The gods were using her brother to talk to each other? But this couldn't be good for Pete. "Help him!" she begged Therese.

"There's something else," Pete—or rather the voice inside Pete—said. "Before he trapped me here, I overheard Zeus give orders for something on Cyclopes Island. That can only mean one thing."

Therese looked up at the other god with a strange expression on her face.

"Therese," Jen pleaded.

"He must be amassing an arsenal of thunderbolts," the other god said.

"You have to stop him," the voice inside Pete warned. "Make it your first priority."

Therese exchanged glances with the golden god. Jen felt like she might be sick if her brother didn't wake up soon.

"Do something," Jen insisted. "Don't let him stay like this."

"Pete?" Jen's mother ran into the barn, followed by Bobby and Mr. Stern. She fell beside Jen, who looked up to see Therese and the golden god had disappeared. "What's happened to him? Another seizure? Bobby, call 9-1-1!"

Bobby went to the old rotary phone on the barn wall and made the call while her mother and Mr. Stern tried to revive Pete. Jen watched on, still dazed by what she'd seen.

*Therese?* Jen prayed. *What's going on? I'm scared to death.*

Therese appeared on her knees beside Jen and wrapped her arms around her. Apparently the others couldn't see her friend.

"He's okay," Therese whispered in a barely audible voice just before she disappeared.

Therese's gesture should have made Jen feel better, perhaps, but it didn't. She was angry that the gods were using her brother in a way that clearly made him sick. And she was determined to make them stop.

***

Than was alarmed when, after Therese and Apollo made their report to Hades, she asked him for a word alone in their rooms.

"What is it?" he asked, anticipating the worst. Maybe she discovered who was fated to die on their wedding day.

She climbed onto his lap and put her arms around his neck. Then she closed her eyes and nestled her face against his throat.

He swallowed hard. He hadn't expected her to fold herself into him and was reminded of how much he missed being alone with her. If only they could have more time like this.

"This feels nice," he whispered and then brushed his lips across her hair.

"I'm worried about Pete," she said.

Talk about a mood buster.

"I think he's obsessed with seeing the future," she added. "I think he needs help."

Than tightened his arms around her and kissed the top of her head. "What do you want me to do?"

"I don't know," she said, burying her face in his chest. "But I was thinking maybe…"

He lifted her chin and looked into her eyes. "Maybe what?"

"Couldn't we ask Tiresias for advice? He's been in Pete's position. Maybe he can tell us how to help Pete."

It actually wasn't a bad idea. "When should we go talk to him?"

"You'll come with me?" She gave him a huge smile. "Thank you! I've only ever gone into the fields once, to see my parents. I wouldn't know the first place to look for him."

"Tiresias isn't in the Elysian Fields."

"What? Where is he?"

"Tartarus."

Therese's mouth dropped open in shock. "Why?"

He wished she hadn't asked, but he couldn't avoid the truth. "That's where all seers who use their gifts to predict the future end up eventually. It's considered an act of pride. Mortals acting like gods. It's one of the worst infractions a person can commit."

"Then why would Hip tell Pete to do it?" The look of disgust on Therese's face made Than stiffen.

"He never told Pete to do it."

"That's not what Pete said."

"He told Pete that blood helps the dead communicate with the living, but he never told Pete to do it," Than said again.

Therese jumped from Than's lap and punched the empty leather chair across from him.

"Hip should have known Pete would try it," she said.

"Don't blame this on my brother," Than said. "Pete still had a choice. Hip even warned him. He told him the same thing I told you. Pete still chose to do it."

"But Pete helped us. Cybele spoke to us through him. That should count for something."

"The same can be said for Tiresias," Than said.

Therese looked across the room at him with a face full of despair. "We have to find a way to save Pete's soul. I can't let him end up in Tartarus forever. You've always said life isn't fair but death is. I don't see how condemning Pete to Tartarus forever is fair."

"Playing god is one of the unpardonable sins."

"We have to help him. Please, Than."

Than went to her and kissed the palm of her hand. He wished he could think of something reassuring to say, but when she threw herself against him and into his arms, all he could do was hug her back.

## CHAPTER EIGHT

# Tartarus

Therese followed Than through the dark, cold corridor that spiraled down, down, down into the pit of Tartarus. The shrieks and wails of tortured souls reached them before she and Than broached the gate, causing her to shudder. The Phlegethon flamed up wildly here, casting shadows overhead. As Than pulled the gate open, the iron scraped along the stone floor and ceiling, and the hinges creaked. Tizzie, hovering over her prisoner, turned at the sound of their entrance.

Tizzie's hair hissed in snakes about her head. Blood dripped from her red sockets. Her dark face was fierce and terrifying. Her wolf, below her on the stone floor, howled.

"We've come to see Tiresias," Than explained.

The prisoner below Tizzie lay stretched across a stone slab. Tizzie held a medicine dropper in one hand, from which a purple, foul smelling liquid dropped against her prisoner's tightly clamped lips. Therese gasped when she looked more carefully at the prisoner. She knew him. It was McAdams, her parents' killer.

Memories of the days when she hunted with the Furies flooded through her. She recalled the face in the window just before her mother was shot leaving Fort Lewis College, the plunge into Huck Finn Pond, the cold water oozing up her body, suffocating her parents and her.

Than led her by the elbow away from Tizzie and the prisoner, further into the deep, cold pit. Far off in the distance, she recognized Sisyphus, who'd been recaptured and who had returned to his task of rolling his rock. He didn't seem to notice her. To her right, she recognized Tantalus and the grapes dangling forever above his reach. His inconsolable moans made her shiver. Apparently you didn't have to be a seer to never make it out of Tartarus to the Elysian Fields.

Soon they came upon Meg, and surprisingly, other gods were with her: Hades, Persephone, Hecate, and Apollo. As Therese and Than neared the group, she recognized Melinoe in the midst of them, chained with her back against a wall, her wrists and ankles shackled. Meg's eyes bled like those of her sister, and her falcon fluttered threateningly near Melinoe's face.

*Are they asking her about Cybele?* Therese asked Than.

*They must be*, he replied. *Let's wait and see what she says.*

Therese was as anxious as Than to know what was going on. Had Melinoe revealed the location of Cybele's prison?

"This could be your chance to redeem yourself," Persephone said in a strained voice. Therese could tell she'd been crying. "If you know anything, please tell us now. Give us a sign that you want to rejoin this family."

Melinoe spat toward the other gods, but the spittle landed ineffectually on the cold stone ground. "Zeus is my family!"

"I'm your mother!" Persephone insisted.

"Go away from me!" Melinoe growled. "I hate you!"

Therese could only imagine what it must be like for Persephone to hear her daughter speak to her like that.

Persephone covered her face and wept.

"Your mother doesn't deserve to be treated this way!" Hades bellowed. "She did nothing but love you!"

Good for Hades for defending his wife, Therese thought. Talk some sense into the Malevolent.

"Is that what you call this?" Melinoe screeched. "Love?"

Meg's voice roared and echoed throughout the pit when she said, "Think on your crimes against humanity!"

Therese shuddered, reminded of the awesome power of the Furies to intimidate and punish.

Hecate took a step daringly close to the prisoner. "Don't you realize no one can lie before Apollo? Did you not hear that your *father* intended to blame you for the attack on Hades and leave you to suffer for all eternity here in this god-forsaken pit?"

"Good!" she screamed. "Leave me and let me suffer in peace!"

What was wrong with this goddess, Therese wondered, that she would prefer to suffer for all eternity than to help her own family?

"There will be no peace for you!" Meg roared.

Her falcon dipped toward Melinoe and plucked out one of her eyes.

Melinoe screamed in agony.

A shiver snaked down Therese's back, and she turned away from the horrible sight. Gertrude, one of the rats she'd befriended in the Underworld, squealed with fear from some crevice and ran up Therese's leg to perch, quivering, on her shoulder.

*Don't be alarmed. You're safe,* Therese told Gertrude.

Persephone covered her face and fled from the pit. Hecate followed her mistress.

That's when Melinoe noticed Therese and said, "You!"

Everyone turned and looked at Therese. She had no idea what to say and stood there, speechless, holding Gertrude in both hands.

"This is your fault!" Melinoe shouted. "If you hadn't gotten involved, I'd be Queen of the Underworld!"

How dare the Malevolent blame Therese! The goddess of ghouls needed to learn to take responsibility for her own choices. Anger surged through Therese, but she took control of it and said in a reasonable voice, "You brought this on yourself, and you're being given a chance to get out of it. You should take it."

Therese turned and walked away, so pissed she couldn't bear to look at the Malevolent for another minute.

Then to Gertrude, she whispered, "It's okay, dearie. There's no danger for you."

"Why should I trust them?" Melinoe called after her. "How do I know they won't…" The Malevolent's voice trailed off.

Therese stopped in her tracks and turned back to face the prisoner. So that's what was keeping her from cooperating. Melinoe had no reason to believe anything anyone told her, because she had trusted her father, and he had betrayed her. She probably still believed that Persephone and Hades had intentionally deceived her about her conception. With no allies, no one to trust, no one to believe in, Melinoe was in despair and lacked the motivation to cooperate. In fact, she was probably terrified that something worse than her imprisonment here might befall her if she betrayed Zeus.

Therese took several steps toward Melinoe, whose one eye glared at her with suspicion and—Therese thought—hope.

Therese's heart rate increased as a new idea struck her. It might be the stupidest thing she'd ever do, but she wanted to do it. She did, didn't she? The other gods seemed transfixed by the glare the two goddesses held on one another—the goddess of ghouls bound to the stone wall and the goddess of animal companions bound to something pulling at her heart, where she clutched Gertrude protectively.

"I swear," Therese began.

Than interrupted, *What are you doing? What are you about to swear? I have a right to know.*

*It's a safe bet*, she replied. *Trust me.*

Aloud, Therese said, "I swear on the River Styx that if any one of these gods before you treats you with injustice, I will join you here, in Tartarus, forever."

Than laid a hand on her shoulder and prayed, *How can you swear such a thing?*

*Do you doubt these gods?* she asked.

Than did not reply.

She looked from Melinoe to Hades and saw a hint of a smile on the god of the Underworld, but suddenly she wasn't quite so sure if it was the same smile of endearment he'd given her before. Had she just made a colossal mistake?

Melinoe spat at her, and this time the spittle hit its mark. Therese flinched.

"Oath breaker!" Melinoe shrieked. "Why should I believe an oath breaker!"

"She never broke an oath," Hades said smoothly.

"She speaks the truth," Apollo added.

"Get away from me!" Melinoe screamed. "All of you! Get away! I want my father! He's coming for me! Just you wait and see! Father! Father, where are you!"

Than took Therese's elbow and led her away from the horrible sight further into the deep pit of Tartarus. Therese pet Gertrude once more before setting her loose on the wall to find her way back to her sisters and brothers.

When they were alone in the dark, winding corridor, spiraling further into the pit, Than asked Therese, "You might not care what happens to you, but what about me?"

"What?"

He took her by the shoulders and gazed down at her. "Don't you care for me and for my happiness?"

"Of course. I love you." He was scaring her. Did he really think any of those gods would act unjustly?

"Except for the Fates, and sometimes Apollo, none of us knows what the future holds. I love my father, and I believe he's just, but you've seen how brothers treat brothers. You've witnessed fathers turn on their sons and daughters."

"Hades is different," Therese said.

"I hope so. But what about Apollo?" he asked.

"He can't lie," she said.

"That doesn't mean he's incapable of injustice."

Nausea crept up Therese's throat.

"Eternity is a very long time, Therese. Things can change. Oaths last forever. Don't be so quick to swear them."

"Well, it's too late now," she said. "What's done is done. We'll just have to trust them. Now where's Tiresias?"

Than muttered with disapproval, "Too late now. Ugh."

"I am here," a voice came from a crack in the stone.

"He's on the other side of this wall," Than said. "Come on."

Than led Therese through a narrow opening and into a large hall where a dim orange light glimmered over the asphodel cascading down the walls. The Phlegethon did not flow here, so consequently, there was little light, though she, being a goddess, could still see. Many souls wandered or sat idly in this part of Tartarus, and the wails, moans, and shrieks could barely be heard.

"It's quiet," Therese whispered.

"The souls in here aren't tormented," Than explained. "Their suffering comes from being separated from the ones they love."

"You mean they have their memories?" Therese asked.

"Yes, but they would be happier without them."

Although the asphodel and the shimmer of light made the hall less dismal than the previous section of Tartarus, it was still nothing like the beauty of the Elysian Fields.

"Tiresias," Than beckoned. "We need a word with you."

***

Mercy Regional Medical Center was packed with people as Jen followed Bobby and Mr. Stern through the psych ward looking for Pete's room. When they found it, Jen's mother was sitting beside the hospital bed where Pete lay sleeping. For the first time, she looked small and fragile to Jen, who'd always seen her mother as the strong horsewoman and taskmaster on their ranch. Her mother stood and put her finger to her lips as they entered. She waved them back out of the room and then led them down the hall to a waiting room.

"Let him get some sleep," Mrs. Holt said. "Sit here with me, and I'll tell you what the doctor said."

Mrs. Holt had ridden in the ambulance with Pete, and Jen had come with Bobby in Mr. Stern's sedan. Mr. Stern had driven like an old man, turning a thirty-minute drive into an hour.

"Sorry it took us so long, Steph," Mr. Stern said. "I'm not used to those country roads, especially at night."

"Don't apologize," Jen's mother said. "I'm grateful you drove the kids over. Neither of them was in any condition to drive."

"I'm fine, Mom," Bobby said. "Just worried."

"Damn, I need a cigarette," she said. "There's an atrium on the floor above us where you can smoke. Do y'all mind?"

Jen wanted to say, "Seriously?" but she held her tongue, knowing this wasn't the best time to pick a fight with her mother. She and her brother followed their mom and Mr. Stern to the elevator where they rode to the next level. In the middle of the floor was a courtyard of sorts open to the cold, dark night. It was windy but at least it wasn't snowing when they bundled their coats more tightly around them and huddled close together on two benches.

Jen's mother took a pack of cigarettes from the pocket of her coat and tapped one out. After she lit it, took a drag, and exhaled, she said, "So the doctors are gonna run some tests on him tomorrow."

"What kind of tests?" Jen asked. She wanted to tell her this was a mistake. Pete wasn't sick. He was a seer. But how would that sound?

"They'll do an MRI and a cat scan, and they'll also do some kind of psych evaluation."

"What's a psych evaluation?" Bobby asked.

Mr. Stern said, "They'll ask him some questions and observe him. It's no big deal, nothing to worry about."

"I told them about my uncle and how schizophrenia runs in our family," Jen's mother continued. "So, they're gonna test him for that, too. The doc says it might take a week or two to get any kind of diagnosis. They'll determine tomorrow whether Pete can come home or if he'll have to remain here during that time."

"He might have to stay here?" Jen asked. "In the hospital?"

"Maybe," her mother said.

Jen wondered if that might be the best thing for him. It would keep him away from her father's ghost—unless the ghost could follow Pete all the way here to Mercy Regional. A quiver moved down her neck.

"I want to stay here with him," Jen said. "I don't want to leave his side, Mom. And you can't make me."

***

Therese took a shaky breath as Tiresias approached. His soul looked old and weary. He wore a white sarong at his waist and no shirt, exposing the transparent appearance of withered flesh, sagging breasts, and hunched shoulders. With a staff in one hand, he walked without opening his phantom eyes.

That's right, Therese thought to herself. Tiresias was blind, even in death.

"Be forewarned," the old soothsayer declared. "I have rarely been believed by those who have sought my knowledge."

"Why?" Therese asked, unable to stop her curiosity from provoking the question.

"The truth hurts," the old man replied. "And I don't like to tell it."

"Then why do you?" she asked.

"It's usually bullied out of me," he said. "And I am a weak, old man."

*Does he really deserve to be here?* She prayed to Than.

Than cleared his throat and said, "We haven't come to ask about the future but to seek advice about a friend—a seer, like you."

"I have no advice for your friend." The old man began to turn away.

"Wait!" Therese said. "Don't go!"

"Stay," Than said. "I command you."

Tiresias stood with his back to them and said, "See how I am bullied?"

Therese plucked an arrow from her quiver, dragged the tip across the palm of her hand, and watched her blood bead to the surface of her skin. Tiresias turned toward her, his nostrils flaring.

"Drink," she offered.

*You didn't have to do that*, Than said. *I could have.*

*What does it matter which of us does it?*

Tiresias lapped up the drops of blood pooling in her hand.

After a few moments, Therese pulled her hand away, wiped it on the side of her pants, and asked, "How can we help Peter Holt stop using his gifts of sight?"

"Why should he stop?" the old man asked.

"Because it's making him sick," Therese replied. "And I don't want him to end up here."

"It's too late for that," Tiresias said. "He's already committed the worst sin of all. And it's only making him sick because he uses his eyes. An eyeless seer sees more easily."

"Do you mean to say blindness would cure him?" Than asked.

"Blindness would ease the physical toll his visions take on his body," the soothsayer explained.

"We can't blind Pete," Therese objected.

The old man shrugged. "No one likes to hear what I have to say."

"How can we get him to stop talking to his father's ghost?" Therese asked.

"Provide him with a motive," Tiresias said.

"Hypnos warned him of the consequences," Than said.

"Not enough." The soothsayer raised a bony finger in the air. "He doesn't care as much about his own well-being as he does that of his family. Everything he asks to see has to do with his mother and siblings. He would suffer for all eternity for them."

"You want us to blind him and threaten the lives of his family?" Therese asked.

"I want neither." The old man lifted his staff and turned to go away. "I want peace."

Therese watched the decrepit soul limp into the darkness.

## CHAPTER NINE

# In Search of Cyclopes Island

Since the day of their contest, Artemis had been standoffish toward Therese, but one day, in late February, the goddess of the hunt sought Therese in her favorite bat cave. The bats had already left to feed, and only the babies had remained behind. Therese had brought Hecate, Galin, and Cubie along to observe the tiny bats and to await the magnificent return of the parents.

"Dione has great respect for you, am I right?" Artemis asked Therese.

Therese glanced at Hecate, wondering what she thought of this comment.

*What's Artemis up to?* Therese asked Hecate.

*I sense she's seeking your help.*

Therese returned her gaze to Artemis. "Dione seemed to like the way I stood up to the gods who wanted me to wear Hippolyta's girdle."

"She is a possible ally none of us have explored," Artemis said.

"But would she side against her own daughter?" Hecate asked.

Therese wasn't sure how Dione would feel about opposing Aphrodite but doubted the Oceanid would want to. And yet, Therese had been snubbed by the goddess of love for so long now that it hurt to even think of her.

"That's what we need to find out." Artemis paced along the cave with her arms crossed at her chest, like a caged lioness.

Cubie, the Doberman, then said, "I would never oppose one of my children, if I could help it."

"But Aphrodite seems neutral," Hecate said. "I don't think she's involved."

Therese gnawed on her lower lip. She really didn't think she'd earned enough respect from Dione to sway her against her own daughter, even if Hecate was right and Aphrodite was neutral, but before Therese could voice this concern, Artemis sat down on a rock and continued to speak.

"Hecate and I have a history with Dione. Did you know that, Therese?"

Therese shook her head.

"I sense a story coming on," Galin said as she curled up in a ball near Artemis's feet. "Wake me up when it's over."

Artemis narrowed her eyes at the polecat, and for a moment, Therese feared the goddess would kick Galin, but Hecate swept her familiar up in her arms and held her in her lap on the far side of the cave. Cubie sat on her haunches beside them.

Therese followed their lead and took a seat on a ledge of rock. "What kind of history?"

"Hecate's mother, Asteria, once turned herself into a quail to avoid Zeus's advances," Artemis explained. "She dived into the sea and became the island known as Delos."

Therese shook her head in disgust. She was sick of these kinds of stories about the king of the gods. How selfish could he be? She knew this behavior was typical among mortal kings and had read enough of human history to recall how many women's lives were destroyed by selfish monarchs—Henry the Eighth being one example. But a god should be better than that.

"So where do you and Dione fit in?" Therese asked Artemis.

"I was born on Delos," Artemis said. "My mother, Leto, is…"

"My mother's sister," Hecate said.

"You two are cousins," Therese recalled. "That's right."

"When Hera discovered that Zeus had gotten Leto pregnant," Artemis continued, "Hera came after her."

"Why doesn't Hera ever go after Zeus?" Therese complained.

"He's too strong for her," Hecate said. "She probably would if she could."

"She did try once, remember?" Artemis said.

Oh yeah, Therese thought. The first binding of Zeus. The one that went terribly wrong.

A nerve twitched below Therese's right eye. "So what did Leto do?"

"She took refuge on Delos and gave birth to me first," Artemis said. "Then I helped her give birth to Apollo. Dione was there, and her sister Amphitrite. They formed a lookout, in case Hera returned, and they promised to protect us from her." Artemis stood from her rock. "Dione has watched my back ever since. She might help us in this mission to find Cyclopes Island."

"What do you mean *find* it?" Therese asked. "Don't you know where it is?" Therese had its location memorized after what had transpired there a few months ago, when she, Than, and the Furies went to borrow Polyphemus's eye.

"Didn't anyone tell you?" Artemis asked. "The island's missing."

***

Hip hesitated outside the gates of Mount Olympus before asking the Seasons to let him enter. Going to Aphrodite had been Than's idea. Hip wasn't so sure it was a good one, given the tension between her and the gods of the Underworld.

Than had argued that Hip's visit would not only divert the Olympians from the activities of the Athena Alliance (as they'd come to call themselves), but also provide Hip with good advice from the goddess of love, who couldn't bear to ignore matters concerning the heart.

Hip entered with wary steps.

Zeus addressed him as soon as Hip broached the great hall.

"I've come to see Aphrodite," Hip explained.

He glanced at Hephaestus and Athena, who pretended not to notice him. Hephaestus sat on his throne tinkering with a toolbox, and Athena was talking with Hestia. Apollo and Artemis were not at home.

"Of course, dear boy," Zeus said. "You are welcome to speak to her."

Hip approached Aphrodite where she sat with her Graces. She refused to meet his eyes.

Feeling hurt and rejected by her, Hip froze in his tracks. "Never mind," he said, turning away. "This was a bad idea."

"Wait," Aphrodite said.

Hip turned back to face her, and she finally met his gaze.

"You're in love with the mortal, Jen Holt," Aphrodite said. "Am I correct?"

He was amazed by how much she was able to sense when it came to matters of the heart. He took several steps closer to the goddess and the three Graces seated beside her, one of whom was Pasithea, his old fiancée. "Yes."

This was way too uncomfortable, discussing his current love in front of an old one. He said as much in prayer to Aphrodite, but she ignored it.

"What would you have me do?" Aphrodite asked.

*Could you send Pasithea on an errand or something? This is awkward.*

Aphrodite simply said, "I'm waiting, Hypnos."

It occurred to Hip that maybe Aphrodite wasn't able to hear his prayers or to answer them.

*Can you even hear me?*

Aphrodite glanced at her father, who was watching them carefully.

Hip decided he should speak. "My problem is this." Hip studied Pasithea before continuing. "I'm afraid I don't have what it takes to commit to one person forever."

In his peripheral vision, Hip could see Pasithea's cheeks redden.

"Hypnos," Aphrodite said gently. "Jen is a mortal. What's this talk of forever?"

"But…"

"Her lifetime will go by in a flash. You will have centuries upon centuries to love again," Aphrodite said.

"But…"

"Surely you can remain loyal to a person for less than one century," the goddess of love added.

The Graces stifled their giggles.

"I hope so," Hip said. "But when she gets all wrinkled and gray…"

Aphrodite jumped to her feet and crossed her arms at her chest. "Hypnos! What are you? A man or a god?"

The Graces giggled more loudly.

"Huh?" Why was she asking? Wasn't the answer obvious?

"Well?" Aphrodite demanded.

"A god, of course."

"Then you must know you have the power to behold the one you love as she appears to you now." She threw her hands in the air. "You can control how you perceive her. So, what's the problem?"

"I can?"

The Graces laughed out loud, which was beginning to piss him off.

"Of course, you can," Aphrodite said.

"I didn't know that."

Aphrodite let her hands drop to her sides and moved closer to Hip. The frustration left her face, and she gave him a gentle smile. "I can see your heart is pure. I can see your love is genuine. I truly believe it is strong enough to last her lifetime."

Hip wondered if that was because Jen was the person fated to die on the summer solstice during Than and Therese's wedding.

Aphrodite took his hands, which surprised him. What surprised him even more was the piece of paper exchanged between them. He hid it in his fist as he kissed the goddess of love on her cheek.

"Thank you, Aphrodite," he said, as she stepped away and returned to her throne. "I feel so much better now." He bowed to her and to the Graces, avoiding Pasithea's eyes.

Then he turned to Zeus and said, "Thank you, Lord Zeus, for allowing me this visit. My heart feels lighter already."

Zeus gave him a subtle nod. Hip turned to leave and felt the eyes of all the gods watching him.

***

Therese and Artemis stood together on the banks of the Black Sea in Turkey, where Dione was known to spend her time. Artemis called to the Oceanid, and within moments, her silver eyes gleamed up at them from the surface of the water.

"We need your help," Artemis said. "We're looking for Cyclopes Island, which seems to have disappeared. Do you know of it?"

Therese admired Artemis's assertive, yet tactful, approach.

"Indeed," the Oceanid replied.

Therese knelt on the sand to better see Dione. "We were wondering if you would go with us to investigate its original location."

"We want to see if a cloak has been placed around it, and if not, we are hoping to find clues as to its whereabouts," Artemis clarified.

Dione's face emerged from the water, silver and shining with excitement. "I would be happy to go with you. Shall we swim or fly?"

"Swim," Therese said. She didn't add that they were hoping to avoid Zeus's notice.

"Follow me." Dione disappeared beneath the sea.

Therese and Artemis dived into the cool water and followed Dione across the Black Sea and through the Bosporus into the Sea of Marmara. Therese had swum these areas before and was proud of her acquired knowledge of the names of the various bodies of water. She also enjoyed swimming for long stretches—miles and miles—and varied her strokes to maximize her enjoyment of it. They hadn't made it far into the Dardanelles Straight when Amphitrite appeared and asked them where they were going.

"We're looking for Cyclopes Island," Artemis answered. "Do you know if a cloak has been placed around it?"

"No cloak," Amphitrite replied. "It's been taken."

"Taken?" Therese folded her arms. Zeus had physically moved the island to another location.

"By whom, dear sister?" Dione asked.

Therese didn't have to ask.

"We're not sure who took it," Amphitrite said. "But it's gone."

"Do you have any idea where?" Artemis asked.

"It is nowhere in the kingdom of the sea," Amphitrite declared. "We've looked everywhere."

"Then it must be hidden in the skies," Dione suggested.

*Great,* Therese prayed to Artemis. *How can we investigate the skies without attracting Zeus's attention?*

"Thank you for your help, Lady Amphitrite," Artemis said. "I suppose we should take a look at the site and check for clues."

"Do you mind if I join you?" the goddess of the sea asked.

"Not at all," Artemis said. "Lead the way."

***

As Than boarded Charon's raft with the souls in his custody, Hecate appeared.

"Your father needs you in his chambers immediately," she said.

Than disintegrated and left with Hecate, curious to learn if there were new developments afoot and trying not to worry that something had gone wrong.

When he arrived in his father's meeting room, Hypnos and his parents were already assembled around a table.

"Has something happened?" Than asked as he took a seat.

Hip was the one who answered him. "I went to see Aphrodite, as you suggested."

"Oh?" Than asked. *So why have a meeting about it?* he prayed privately to Hip.

"She gave me this." Hip handed him a small, folded piece of paper.

Than carefully unfolded it. Written inside were the words, "Help me."

Than studied each of the faces around the table. "What do you think this means? Is she in danger?"

"We were hoping you could tell us," Persephone said. "Of all of us, you have been particularly close to her lately."

"She's been ignoring me ever since Therese used her as a diversion when we rescued Artemis and Hephaestus from Mount Olympus."

Hades rubbed his beard and sighed. "We need to determine whether she truly needs our help, or whether Zeus intends to use her as his spy."

"How do we do that?" Hip asked.

Than was wondering the same thing.

"I have an idea," Persephone said. "If Therese asks Aphrodite to be her matron of honor and the Graces to be her bridesmaids…"

"Mother, please," Than interrupted. "She's the least experienced god." And they were relying on Therese too much, in Than's opinion.

"You don't have faith in her abilities?" Hades challenged.

"Of course, I do," Than said.

"Then it's settled," Hades said. "As soon as Therese returns from her mission with Artemis, bring her to me so we can hatch the plan."

***

After searching underwater where Cyclopes Island used to be, Therese felt like a failure. They had found nothing to indicate what had happened, and none of the creatures they had questioned had any knowledge of its whereabouts. They all described the same phenomenon Amphitrite had already mentioned: There had been a loud rumbling, the earth and sea had quaked for a few moments, then a great current had sucked everything for miles toward the spot once occupied by land. Eventually everything had settled back to normal.

The four goddesses were about to give up their investigation when Callisto appeared, flapping her hands with excitement.

"I have news!" she said. "I was visiting my son, Arcas, last night—you know, Little Bear?"

"What news?" Artemis asked.

"I didn't put it together until just now." Callisto lifted her arms above her head in a dramatic gesture of enlightenment.

"Put what together?" Therese asked.

"He said there was a massive cloud that hadn't moved for days," Callisto explained. "He's been watching it with interest, expecting it to unleash a deluge. He called it a marvel. He's never seen anything like it on Earth."

Therese arched a brow. "So, you think the cloud may contain…"

"Cyclopes Island," Dione said.

"Where is it?" Artemis asked.

"Arcas said it's floating above the Arctic Ocean somewhere between Greenland and Iceland," Callisto said.

"That's the Denmark Straight," Amphitrite said. "I know precisely where that is. Shall we go?"

Therese's heart picked up speed at this new prospect of finding the island.

"Hold on." Artemis looked from Amphitrite to Dione.

*Aren't we in a hurry?* Therese prayed privately to Artemis.

"I need you both to swear an oath on the River Styx."

*Ah, smart move. What about Callisto?* Therese prayed again.

*She's already sworn her allegiance to me.*

"Not here," Dione said. "We need to go on land. Sound travels for miles underwater, and we can easily be overheard."

"Where should we go?" Therese asked.

"We're not too far from my sacred temple in Ephesus," Artemis said. "It's heavily warded. Let's go there."

The four other goddesses followed Artemis across the Aegean Sea along the coast of Turkey toward Ephesus. Once on land, they ran, in invisibility mode, to the temple ruins. Tourists strolled along the grounds, but Artemis knew of a secret cavern beneath them where they could speak without distractions and, more importantly, without being overheard by other gods.

"I need to know that I can trust you," Artemis said. "What I have to say is about standing up for goddesses who have been treated unjustly and whose voices continue to be suppressed."

"I love it," Dione said with a smile.

"You speak of our sister, Metis?" Amphitrite asked.

"First swear," Therese said. "Swear you'll tell no one what we are about to reveal to you."

"Swear on the River Styx," Artemis clarified.

"I swear on the River Styx," Dione said, without hesitation.

Everyone looked at Amphitrite.

"It sounds like you're asking me to commit treason against our king," Amphitrite said.

Therese's heart pounded wildly with anticipation. She hoped they hadn't made a mistake in including Amphitrite.

"We believe he's the one responsible for hiding Cyclopes Island," Artemis said. "We suspect he's building an arsenal of thunderbolts."

"But why?" Amphitrite asked.

Artemis told them about Pete's prophecy.

"He's going to use my wedding for his attack," Therese explained.

Therese went on to tell them about Cybele and Melinoe, and added, "So you see, your sister isn't the only goddess we need to save."

"If we don't stand up against this patriarchal tyrant," Artemis began, "our rights may be the next to be stripped away."

"He can't continue to use women for his own pleasure, and then abuse them when it suits his needs," Therese added.

"We aren't the only ones who feel this way," Artemis said. "We want you to join us, but first you have to swear on the River Styx to tell no one of our plan."

Amphitrite raised her right hand and placed it over her heart. "I swear on the River Styx to keep this plan to myself."

***

After her mom and Bobby had left, Jen sat in Pete's hospital room at Mercy Regional and slipped the dream globe from her coat pocket. Pete had been in a coma for three weeks. The psych evaluation had to be postponed, but all of the other tests had revealed nothing. When Jen communicated with Hip through the globe, he had tried to cheer her up by saying that Pete was better off in the coma. She had begun to suspect Hip was the reason Pete hadn't been able to wake up.

To make matters worse, Pete hadn't been dreaming, so she had been unable to use the globe to gain insight into his head.

Undeterred, she focused on the globe and silently asked to see Pete's dream. Although nothing happened for several long minutes, at some point, when she had nearly forgotten and had begun to daydream about Hip, the globe lit up like a Christmas tree, and distorted sounds and images followed.

Worried she might be entering someone else's night-time adventures, she whispered, "Show me Pete's dream."

The colors and images swirled like a hurricane. One by one, like the rolling credits at the end of a movie, the faces of people she knew appeared and disappeared: Therese, Than, and herself, and each of their family members stared back at her from the globe. She even saw Ray and Todd and other friends. They were dressed in nice clothes. And then it dawned on her.

Pete was dreaming about Therese's wedding day.

This ought to be good, she thought.

In a beautiful wedding gown, Therese walked across the gravel pad on Richard's arm. The sun was shining, red birds were chirping, and a beautifully decorated arbor had been set up at the end of the aisle, where Than stood waiting. But something was wrong. The images shimmered, and a shout sounded from the globe. It was Pete.

"No!" he shouted again.

So maybe Pete was still in love with Therese after all, Jen thought. That would explain why he was having a dream about her wedding day, and why the dream was quickly turning into a nightmare.

The sudden appearance of her father's ghostly face scared her, and she nearly dropped the globe on the hospital room floor.

"Pete!" the ghost moaned in a ghoulish voice that was only faintly like her father's. "If Therese marries the god of death, the lord of Mount Olympus will fall, and your sister will perish."

This time Jen did drop the globe. It fell on its side and rolled beneath the bed.

CHAPTER TEN

# Revelations

Therese watched in amazement as Amphitrite's daughter, Kym, rose toward them from the depths of the Aegean Sea in the form of a raving current that shoved everything out of its path for miles. When Kym reached the surface, she became a massive tidal wave that threatened the coast of Turkey. Amphitrite gave the signal, and all five goddesses dived into the wave.

Kym, the goddess of storm waves, lifted them up and changed directions, away from the coast of Turkey toward Iceland. They travelled across the Mediterranean, into the Atlantic, and then turned north toward the Arctic Circle.

*No humans or animals will be injured or killed by this mission, right?* Therese asked Artemis.

*We shall see,* came the goddess's cryptic reply.

As they neared Iceland, Kym's husband, Briareos the storm giant, lunged from the sea and created a bank of black, ominous storm clouds that stretched for miles across the Arctic. Amphitrite cloaked Therese, Artemis, Callisto, Dione, and herself in a thick rain cloud, and then the five goddesses leapt from the crest of Kym and into the sky beside Briareos.

To distract any gods who might be watching, Kym changed directions and crawled along the Atlantic to the south toward the equator. Briareos followed, leaving scattered clouds in his wake to camouflage the goddesses, but this made it impossible for them to discern which cloud had been spotted by Arcas. Amphitrite asked Briareos to burst his clouds over the Arctic, and this caused a blizzard to snow down below them. Once the storm-giant's clouds had all dispersed, the goddesses could finally see the enormous black cloud sitting directly above the Denmark Straight.

They sailed below the cloud so that their own might appear indistinct from it. Then the five goddesses reached their hands up through the condensation and felt that, indeed, a solid mass was hidden inside.

Artemis went first, to check it out, before beckoning the other goddesses to follow.

*You won't believe what I see*, Artemis said to them.

When she reached Artemis's side, Therese's mouth fell open. Polyphemus sat on a hill with an icicle hanging from his crying eye. He broke off the icicle and threw it in a rage in the snow, only to watch another form with his tears.

*Why is he sobbing?* Callisto asked.

Therese scoured the icy hills, searching for an answer. A mound of thunder bolts lay beside the weeping Cyclops. The sound of a distant forge echoed through the blustery sky. The sheep bellowed as they wandered across their ice-covered fields. What would make a mean and nasty cannibal cry?

***

Jen paced the floor of her brother's hospital room, banging her fists against her thighs. Should she even go to Therese's wedding? What if the prophecy came true? She sighed and paced and banged her fists some more. How could she not go to her best friend's wedding?

"Jen?"

At first, she thought Pete was waking from his coma, but then she recognized Hip's voice. It came from the globe, which had rolled beneath Pete's bed. Although she was frightened of it, she crouched on the floor and fished the globe out.

"Hey," she said to Hip.

"What's wrong?" he asked.

"You don't know?" she challenged.

"Know what? What's happened?" Hip asked through the globe.

"I saw Pete's dream. I know about the prophecy."

Hip's concerned face transformed to understanding as his pinched brows relaxed. So, he *had* known.

She narrowed her eyes at the glass. "When were you going to tell me about it?"

"Honestly? Never."

She wanted to throw the globe across the room. Maybe he didn't care as much about her as he had led her to believe. "Why not? Didn't you think I should know?"

"What good would that have done anyone?"

"Seriously?"

"Seriously." Hip looked at her blankly.

"Well, for one, I could have started spending every moment I have with my loved ones instead of dreaming about you all day and night."

He looked hurt by that last comment. She'd wanted to hurt him, but now she felt bad.

"I'm sorry," she said. "I know you were trying to keep me from freaking out."

"It's driving all of us crazy," he said. "Trying to guess who the poor soul will be."

"What are you talking about?" Jen asked.

"What are *you* talking about?" Hip said, his face full of confusion.

"The message my father's ghost gave to Pete," Jen clarified.

"Which was…"

"He said on the day Therese marries death, the lord of Mount Olympus will fall, and I will perish," Jen said.

Hip's brows shot up and disappeared beneath his hair. "You? That's not what I was told."

"What were you told?"

"That someone close to Therese would die. That's why I didn't tell you. No name was given."

"But I heard him—my father—say it to Pete in his dream," Jen said, trying to control her trembling hands. "He said *I* would perish."

"That wasn't your father's ghost," Hip insisted. "That was a figment. You can't take what happens in the Dreamworld at face value, and you certainly can't believe it."

But sometimes dreams were prophetic. Even Jen had once had a dream that she'd failed her chemistry test, and the very next day she did. Of course, it hadn't taken a dream to know it would happen. "Then why do people's dreams sometimes come true?"

"There are two kinds of dreams, and each passes through a different gate—one of ivory and the other of horn. The one you saw in the globe was a false dream, because it came through the ivory gate. It's not to be trusted, Jen. Do you hear me?"

"How do you know?" She wanted to believe him, but she worried he was just trying to make her feel better.

"Seriously?"

He appeared in the hospital room beside her. Before she could react, she yawned. It was half-yawn and half-smile. She found the energy to stand as Hip wrapped his arms around her. He smelled fresh and felt warm. His solid arms around her made her feel safe. She yawned again and relaxed against him. Then he disappeared, and she nearly fell on the floor.

As she staggered to her chair, he appeared again in the globe.

"Thanks," Jen said. "I needed that."

"So did I. It wasn't enough. Not nearly enough."

Jen let out a heavy sigh and closed her arms around her.

"Listen," Hip said. "I'm sorry I didn't tell you about the prophecy."

"I don't understand why they don't just call off the wedding. I mean, if someone's going to die, why get married?"

Hip rubbed his chin. "First of all, they are in danger of being imprisoned by Zeus regardless of whether or not they have the wedding. Now that he's heard the prophecy, Zeus won't take any chances."

Therese was in danger, and the only reason Zeus knew of the prophecy was because her brother had told him. "So, it's Pete's fault," she muttered.

"Well, I wouldn't say that."

"Because you're too kind." Her stomach suddenly felt queasy.

"Trust me when I say this is a complicated situation and the chances of a favorable outcome are higher if we go ahead with the wedding."

Jen narrowed her eyes. "Favorable for whom?"

Hip didn't reply, but he didn't have to. She already knew the answer. In the short time she'd known the gods she'd come to realize that the needs of humans were rarely their top priority.

***

Than searched the sea for signs of Therese and Artemis as he flew with his souls from a sunken ship, but he saw no sign of them. Why hadn't they answered his prayers?

*Therese? Where are you?* He reached out again.

*Sorry,* she finally replied. *The tidal wave had me too flustered.*

*What tidal wave?*

*You won't believe what we've discovered,* she rattled on. *We've found the island. It's hidden by a cloud above the Denmark Straight.*

Than disintegrated and flew toward that location. *I'm on my way.*

*Don't. You'll attract attention.*

Therese was right. He didn't want to be seen by Zeus. He hovered several miles away and used his excellent vision to investigate the region. Thick, dark clouds gathered above the straight.

*Are you in the middle of those clouds?* he asked.

*Amphitrite cloaked us. Dione and Callisto are with us as well. You won't believe what Polyphemus is doing. I actually feel sorry for him. Zeus is horrible for making him do it. We have to stop him.*

Before Than could ask what Therese meant, a flash of lightning struck. It lit up the clouds with a halo of fire before fading into a thunderous roar. Then, like eagles toward their prey, the five goddesses fell toward the sea. Than god travelled to them, but they plunged into the water like cannons before he could catch them.

He struck through the water and disintegrated into five, each racing after a goddess toward the bottom of the sea. Although he managed to reach Callisto, Artemis, and Therese, a swarm of sharks circled protectively around Amphitrite and Dione, and when he tried to pass, they opened their jaws threateningly.

"I want to help them," he said to them. "I swear on the River Styx."

With his oath, the sharks allowed him to pass—they must not have heard he was an oath breaker—and he took the two sea goddesses. Then all five of him made a bee line for Poseidon's Palace, all the while praying to the other gods for help.

He wished he could god travel, but he wouldn't dare risk the safety of the goddesses, so he swam as hard as he could though the Atlantic toward Morocco. He turned east through the Mediterranean Sea and cut through the Strait of Messina toward the Ionian Sea, but as soon as he did, he was sorry. He had forgotten about Scylla and Charybdis and their hatred for Amphitrite. Charybdis sucked in a mouthful of water and then blew it out in a powerful whirlpool that tossed him and the five goddesses toward the rocks off the coast of Italy. Scylla, with her six long necks and grisly heads and her twelve dangling legs, lurched from her cave and pounced on him and Amphitrite. Her claws dug into his skin, sending sharp pains up his arms and legs.

Than held fiercely to the goddesses, who remained limp in his arms, as he struggled against Scylla's attack. Scylla's yelping cries pierced his eardrums. He cried out with rage against her and knocked her back toward the rocky bank. She recovered and lunged toward him, but before she reached him, Poseidon emerged in his chariot, and Than—all five of him—leapt into the golden seat behind Poseidon with the goddesses in tow.

"To my palace!" the god of the sea shouted to his three white steeds.

Than had never been so glad to see Poseidon.

Riptide, Seaquake, and Crest charged through the straight, across the Ionian Sea, around the southernmost tip of Greece, and, at last, into the Aegean.

Apollo met them in his chariot at the palace entrance. The gods quickly swam into one of Poseidon's private chambers where they stretched the goddesses onto couches, weighting down Artemis, Callisto, and Therese to keep them from floating away. Than knew they were not close to death, but he feared their paralysis could be permanent.

"They were paralyzed by a direct hit from Zeus," Than explained to Apollo. "Can you help them?"

While Apollo worked his magic on each of the goddesses, Poseidon questioned Than.

"Why would my brother attack my wife and these others?"

Than noted the ferocity in Poseidon's eyes.

"They were investigating the disappearance of Cyclopes Island."

"And did they find anything?" Poseidon asked.

Than told him what he knew.

"Did they discover why my son was so distraught?" Poseidon asked.

"Yes, but they were struck before Therese could tell me."

Poseidon lifted his trident and roared, unleashing his ferocity. The earth shook.

"Please, Lord Poseidon!" Than shouted, though he was afraid. "You'll draw suspicion to us." That was all they needed: Zeus noticing the quaking of the Aegean Sea on the heels of his strike.

Poseidon quieted down but turned his back to Than and paced angrily around the room. Than stepped away to give the god of the sea some private time. He was relieved to see the goddesses stirring.

"Than?" Therese called to him from across the room, and, with his boulder in the crook of his arm, he went to her.

***

Therese blinked several times before she realized she was underwater. Where was she? She looked around but couldn't move her arms and legs.

"Than?" she called, hoping he was nearby.

When he reached her side, he held her hair from floating in her eyes. "Therese? Are you okay?"

"I can't move. I think I was struck by Zeus."

He nodded. "I saw it happen."

"What about the others?" she asked.

"They're awake now too. Soon you'll all be healed. It just takes time."

Now she knew how he had felt four months ago when he had lain paralyzed by Zeus's thunderbolt in the cave at the base of Mount Ida. A dull ache penetrated her muscles. She could lift her head and wiggle her fingers and toes, but that was the extent of her mobility.

He kissed her forehead, and a wave of warmth circulated throughout her body.

"Tell me what you saw," he said.

"Poor Polyphemus," Therese said.

Poseidon moved nearer to the couch where she lay. "Is he Zeus's prisoner, then?"

Therese looked up at the fierce god. "The Cyclopes are creating an arsenal of thunderbolts, and Polyphemus is being forced to..." Therese's voice trailed off.

From her couch, Artemis said, "He's being made to cut open the bellies of his sheep and hide the thunderbolts inside. Then he has to sew them back up."

Poseidon narrowed his eyes. "There must be more to it than that, to make the giant weep."

Therese closed her eyes. "A while back, when we needed his eye to save Persephone and Athena, I shot him with my arrow to make him love his sheep."

Amphitrite licked her lips. "We heard him tell his sheep that he would never fling them to the ground, as he's been ordered."

"He's afraid of Zeus's wrath," Dione explained. "Polyphemus wants to protect his sheep at his own peril."

"Can't you reverse the effects of your arrow on my son?" Poseidon asked Therese.

"I could," she allowed. "But I have a better idea."

CHAPTER ELEVEN

# Homecoming

Two weeks passed before Therese and the other goddesses regained mobility in their arms and legs, and it was another week before Therese felt she was completely back to normal. The best explanation for their long recovery was that Zeus must have used several thunderbolts at once to knock the goddesses from the sky. Than told her she was lucky to have recovered at all. He knew of a wood nymph who would remain paralyzed forever. Artemis took mercy on her and turned her into a tree so she could at least have a sense of purpose.

Poseidon had made Therese comfortable in a room of her own in his palace. She spent her weeks lying in a soft bed of silk, loosely packed with sand, the most comfortable mattress she'd ever slept on. More than once, she played her flute, and Poseidon asked if he could sit near her bed and listen. Her bed faced two enormous windows shaped like clam shells, and on the other side of them the colorful marine life passed by. She had never before realized how busy the underwater world actually was until she had watched it for days, full of fascination. Despite the pleasure she took in seeing the dolphins, sharks, starfish, stingrays, crabs, sea horses, and vast range of various other fish species, she was anxious to get out of the water and onto dry land. She'd loved the water all her life and had been swimming since the age of two, but after living in it nonstop for three weeks, she was ready to leave it for a while.

Plus, it had been awkward lying beneath the heavy blankets that were necessary to keep her from floating away. Even worse was the pruning of her skin. How the skin of Dione, Amphitrite, and the merfolk managed to look so smooth and wrinkle-free, Therese could not imagine, for her own looked like a three-dimensional road map.

But the worst part of living underwater was the panic that overcame her each time she woke up. It would take her a moment to recall that she could breathe underwater, and there would be this terrifying few seconds, reminiscent of the day her parents died, that would overcome her. Twice, Rhode, a mermaid and another daughter of Amphitrite and Poseidon, rushed to her side to calm Therese down. Rhode helped her by carrying her up to an island where she could sunbathe beneath Helios, Rhode's husband.

When Than arrived in Hades's chariot to pick her up, she was glad to be finally going home, but she would miss her room in Poseidon's palace and its beautiful view. After she said goodbye to Poseidon and each of the goddesses, Artemis reminded her that although they had been struck, they had succeeded in their mission.

"We didn't fail," Artemis said.

"I know," Therese said. "We did good."

"Stay in touch," Dione called out to her.

"I will," Therese said.

"Come back and visit me again soon," Amphitrite said.

"I promise," Therese replied.

She turned to Callisto. "Be sure to thank Arcas. If it hadn't been for him, we might not have found Cyclopes Island."

"Thanks, Therese," Callisto said. "I'll tell him."

Swift and Sure drove Therese and Than in the chariot from the bottom of the Aegean Sea to its surface and then down through the great chasm into the Underworld. The chariot ride filled Therese with a thrill even as she felt a bit sorry to leave the sea.

Once they were in their rooms and had visited with their animals, Than took Therese by the hand and led her to their bedroom.

"I don't want to sleep anymore," Therese said. "I've been in bed for three weeks."

Than smiled, and his eyes glistened. "I didn't bring you in here to sleep."

He pressed his lips hard against hers, and moved his fingers through her hair, which was still wet and curly from the sea. Then he cupped his hands around her neck and held her lips against his. His hot breath sent chills down her spine, and she was overcome with euphoria. Tears of happiness sprang to her eyes as she pressed her hands against his back, reminding herself that this magnificent man belonged to her. She sometimes couldn't believe it.

"Oh, Than," she gasped.

He lifted her up in his arms and carried her to the bed, where he gently laid her down. He moved beside her and gazed down at her—she on her back and he on his side, propped on an elbow. He kissed her again, and she kept her eyes open this time, watching his beautiful face make love to her face. When he opened his eyes and met hers, she blushed and smiled, like a child caught with the cookie jar.

"I love you so much," she said.

He kissed her again and then whispered, against her lips, "I wish we were married."

"It won't be long now." She reached up and kissed his throat three times before lying back down and gazing up at him.

"It's an eternity away."

She laughed, suspecting his notion of eternity to be much longer than hers.

He brushed back her damp hair and covered her face in a flurry of kisses before falling on her and nestling his face against her ear.

"I love you so much, too," he whispered.

Therese closed her eyes and sighed and wished they could lay there like that forever.

***

When Dr. Norton, a petite brunette with large black eyes, returned to Pete's room at Mercy Regional with Pete in a wheelchair, Jen and her mother stood up.

"Don't be alarmed by the chair," the doctor said. "It's standard procedure."

"Well, how did it go?" Jen's mother asked.

The doctor turned down the brakes on the wheelchair and said, "Why don't we all sit down."

That didn't sound good, Jen thought as she and her mother sat on the edge of the hospital bed while the doctor pulled over a stool and sat down.

"As you know," Dr. Norton began. "We found no physical evidence of anything unusual, but our psych evaluation has me concerned."

"Just ask her," Pete said.

"Ask who what, Pete?" Jen's mom asked.

"Ask Jen about the gods," Pete said. "She'll tell you I ain't crazy."

Jen couldn't believe it. Pete had told the doctor Therese's secret. Jen wanted to stand up and kick him in the shin. "Pete! Stop talking like that!"

"But Dad's ghost said…"

"Your father's dead," Jen's mom said gently. She stood up and took Pete's hand. "I'm so sorry your dad is gone, sweet boy. I feel like his death has been the hardest on you."

"Mom, it ain't that," Pete said. "He's been trying to tell me something."

"Calm down, Pete," Dr. Norton said. "Mrs. Holt, please sit down. Let me tell you what I need to say."

"Should we speak privately, doctor?" Mrs. Holt hinted.

"We will," the doctor agreed. "But I want Pete to hear this. I've already told him, but I want him to hear it again. He seems to be suffering from Delusional Disorder."

"What is that?" Mrs. Holt asked.

"It's a psychosis in which the patient sees or believes things which aren't true."

Oh, no, Jen thought. Her brother had a psychosis? Maybe the doctor was wrong. Maybe she just didn't understand about the gods and ghosts and everything.

"Just ask Jen," Pete said. "She'll tell you everything I said is true."

Dr. Norton continued. "In Pete's case, he seems to suffer from a mix of what we call grandiose and persecutory. Patients with Grandiose Delusional Disorder have an over-inflated perception of themselves as a powerful being, usually in response to a traumatic feeling of helplessness. Pete believes he is a seer who can talk to ghosts to learn about the future."

"Pete!" Jen's mother stood up again. "Is that true?"

"Hip told me I'm a seer," Pete said. "I didn't make that up. I swear."

Jen couldn't stand to see her brother suffering. "Hip did tell him that," Jen admitted. "I was there. And I do believe he can talk to Daddy's ghost. There are people on television who do it, and they aren't considered delusional. I saw someone on *Oprah* once."

Jen's mom sat back down, looking a bit pale in the face.

"That's true, Jen," Dr. Norton said. "But they don't have seizures and become comatose. Pete's psychosis is making him physically ill. And his insistence that the Greek gods of ancient myth live and breathe today, well, that makes him different from the so-called mediums you've seen on TV."

But Jen knew the gods were real. How could she say so without sounding crazy herself?

"Jen, tell them about Hip and Than and Therese," Pete insisted.

"Therese?" Jen's mom asked.

Great. Why wouldn't Pete shut up?

"The second type of Delusional Disorder Pete suffers from is called persecutory. That describes the delusional patient who believes he or someone he knows is in danger. Pete believes that someone close to his friend Therese will die on her wedding day.”

“That’s what Dad told me,” Pete said. “You’ve got to believe me.”

Jen wanted to tell her brother to be quiet, but it was too late. The cat was out of the bag. She should probably say something to defend him, but she couldn’t think of anything that wouldn’t make her sound crazy, too.

“I want to believe you, son.” Mrs. Holt turned to the doctor. “So what do we do? How do we help him?”

“For now, we need to keep him calm, so I’m writing a script for a mild sedative. This disorder is sometimes temporary, so I want you to come back to see me in six weeks so I can examine him again.”

“Of course,” Mrs. Holt said.

“Meanwhile, if his symptoms get worse,” Dr. Norton said, “call or bring him in.”

Jen’s mom nodded and smiled at the doctor, but Jen could tell she was holding back the floodgates. Jen’s heart ached for her mother, who thought Pete was sick, and for her brother, whom she had failed to defend. If she had told them what she knew of the Greek gods and her father’s ghost, would they have put her on medication, too?

During the ride home from the hospital, Pete wouldn’t look at her or talk to her. It was clear he felt betrayed. She didn’t blame him. She was as angry with herself as he was. But the best plan of action hadn’t been clear to her—still wasn’t clear to her. She had to find a way to protect her brother and the identity of her best friend at the same time.

She had decided not to tell Pete about what she saw in his dream—about her being named by her father’s ghost as the one fated to die. If the dream had passed through the gates of ivory, and was a lie, then there was no reason to bring it up to her brother, whose state of mind was already fragile.

After she and Bobby had turned out the horses and she had showered and gotten ready for bed, she lay beneath her covers unable to sleep. She started to call to Hip but then thought better of it. She threw off her covers and went down the hall to Pete's room with tears welling in her eyes.

She tapped at the door. When he didn't answer, she opened it. He lay there staring at the ceiling.

"Pete?"

"What do you want?"

He sounded normal, at least. She was relieved that he hadn't been in a trance, or worse. "I want to tell you I'm sorry."

He continued to stare at the ceiling.

"I didn't know what to do," she said.

He still didn't respond.

"I think it's easier for Mom to think you're a little delusional than for her to hear the truth," she said. "It's just too much for her—too much for most people."

He sighed, which was something. At least he wasn't cussing her out.

"So, I guess I'm asking if you can do this for me, if you can handle being misunderstood, so we can protect Mom and Bobby and the others from the truth, and maybe protect Therese's secret, too."

He turned to meet her gaze. She couldn't tell what he was going to say. His face was expressionless. *Go to hell* was just as possible as *I love you.*

"Can you, Pete?"

He closed his eyes and nodded. He didn't open them again. In fact, he looked like he had gone to sleep. Maybe it was the medication.

"Pete?" she asked softly. When he didn't respond, she tip-toed across the room and kissed him lightly on the top of his head. She wished she could go back in time and remove this burden. He had already carried a heavy one for her when he had stood up for her against their father. She leaned over, caught her tear before it landed on him, and whispered, "You're the best big brother in the whole wide world."

***

Than held Therese in his arms, wishing he hadn't promised his parents to tell her as soon as she had returned from Poseidon's palace. His parents had wanted him to tell her while she was still there recuperating, but Than had insisted that Therese be allowed to recover without the extra worry. His parents had honored his request on the condition that as soon as she returned, he would broach the subject.

And now, even though all he wanted was to kiss and hold her, it was time.

He kissed her softly on her ear once more and whispered, "I have news. I need to tell it to you."

Her eyes popped open, and she lifted herself up on both elbows. "What's happened?"

He sat up and squared himself to her. "Aphrodite passed a secret message to Hip when he went to visit her last month."

Therese sat all the way up now. "What did it say?"

"It said, *Help me.*"

She stood from the bed and paced around the room. "I knew it! I knew she couldn't be angry with us forever. I bet she hasn't even been shunning us! I bet Zeus blocked her somehow. Maybe she hasn't even been able to hear our prayers!" She swung around to face Than, her eyes shining bright. "Am I right?"

"Perhaps. We don't know. The note could be a set up. Zeus may have put her up to it."

"I don't believe it."

Than climbed from the bed and took her hand. "We have to consider the possibility. It would be unwise to ignore it. Now come here."

He brought her back to his arms and stroked her hair, which was dry and curlier than she usually fixed it. He never understood why she frequently wore it straight when it was just as beautiful in its natural state.

"There's more," he said. "Hades and Persephone want you to go to Mount Olympus."

"Me?"

He nodded.

"And you didn't fight them on this?" She gave him a wry smile.

He kissed the smile off her lips. "It crossed my mind."

"What am I supposed to do?"

The eagerness in her voice brought a chuckle to his throat. How brave his darling was. It made him proud.

"Persephone thinks you should ask Aphrodite to be your matron of honor and her Graces to be your bridesmaids. That will allow you to spend time with her on Mount Olympus as they help you prepare for the wedding."

Therese frowned.

"What's wrong?" he asked. "I thought you would like the idea."

"I do, but what about Jen?"

"What *about* her?" Than had no idea how Jen was even relevant to the discussion.

"I asked her to be my maid of honor."

A sharp pain pressed against Than's temple, but he willed it away. "Oh no. Will she understand if you ask her to step down?"

Therese's entire body deflated and folded in on itself. He felt it happen in his arms. He lifted her chin and waited for her to meet his gaze. "Have the both of them. You can have them both, can't you?"

"Will Aphrodite be offended, sharing the position of honor?"

"There's only one way to find out."

"On second thought…" Therese pulled away from him and crossed her arms as she paced the room. "Maybe it would be better for Jen if she wasn't at the wedding at all."

CHAPTER TWELVE

# A Week at Mount Olympus

It felt good to be on Stormy's back with Clifford at her side as they answered the prayers of humans and their animal companions. As Therese spent the next few days diligently at work, she thought of how she would approach the goddess of love.

She planned to wait to go to Mount Olympus on the first day of spring when both Persephone and Demeter returned to their double throne among the other Olympians. Persephone had already sent Hecate to secure Poseidon's permission for the use of his spa in his chambers on Mount Olympus. They hoped for an opportunity to spend time with Aphrodite away from Zeus's watchful eyes.

Therese was reminded of the night before she faced McAdams in the ring around the gods. Most of the gods and goddesses had felt sorry for her, like they had expected her to lose, and they had showered her with gifts. Even Zeus had invited her to take a ride on Pegasus. She had been amazed by the clamshell tub in Poseidon's Olympian chambers—she hadn't yet seen his palace, or she would have better understood then why he spent the majority of his time under the sea.

When the first day of spring arrived, she sat with Cubie, Galin, and Hecate in the backseat of the golden chariot waiting for Persephone and Hades. She and Than had already said their goodbyes, but the king and queen of the Underworld needed more time.

Therese could hear them in the corridor just outside the garage.

"You'd think I'd be used to it by now, but I never am," Hades murmured.

"Neither am I, my love," Persephone whispered. "Come visit as often as you can."

"We'll see each other at the wedding if not before," Hades promised.

Then came the sounds of tears and of kissing. At last they both emerged and took their places behind Swift and Sure.

The ride was quiet and solemn. Persephone's entire body shook with each sob. Therese hadn't realized before now how hard Persephone's move to Mount Olympus was on her and Hades each spring.

When they reached the gates and the Seasons, Hades gave Persephone one more embrace before climbing back into the chariot. Though the goddesses and Hecate's familiars watched him drive away, the lord of the Underworld did not look back. Therese felt sure it wasn't callousness that kept him from glancing at them for one final farewell; rather, he did not wish them to see the tears that were likely rolling down his cheeks.

In addition to the sadness of having to witness these two lovers part, Therese was overcome with apprehension. So many things could go wrong during her visit to Mount Olympus. She had been invited by Persephone to stay a week so that they could meet with Aphrodite and her Graces to plan the wedding. She'd been told that Algaea (Hephaestus's secret wife) was the goddess of adornment and grace. Euphrosyne was responsible for good cheer, merriment, joy, and mirth. Thalia crafted festive celebrations and luxurious banquets. And the youngest Grace, Pasithea, Hip's old fiancée, kept everyone calm and relaxed. Although Therese was glad to have their help, she still did not know whether or not she could trust them. She would have to watch her every word.

On the other hand, if Aphrodite's plea for help was sincere, which was what Therese most believed—or wanted to believe—she needed to find out why. What if the goddess of beauty was in danger?

As soon as the goddesses entered the great hall, Zeus and Hera greeted them from their double throne. Demeter had already arrived, and she now rushed to embrace her daughter.

"At last," Demeter said. "It was the longest winter yet."

Persephone's smile seemed forced but not without warmth as she followed her mother across the court to her place between Artemis and Hestia. Artemis sat restringing her bow. Hestia and two of her maidens were working with Athena on quilt squares. Ares, Hermes, and Poseidon were not present, but Apollo played his lyre in the company of four singing Muses, and Hephaestus sharpened an elegant sword.

Aphrodite sat across from Hephaestus with her four Graces. With her bags in tow, Therese crossed the hall to them and curtseyed.

"Hello, Aphrodite." Therese smiled and nodded at each of the Graces, though she only recognized Pasithea and Algaea. She wasn't sure yet which was Thalia and which was Euphrosyne.

Aphrodite glanced toward her father before returning her gaze to Therese. "Hello. Welcome to Mount Olympus."

"Thank you," Therese replied. "I'm glad to be here."

Therese then followed Hecate behind Demeter and Persephone's double throne into the rooms where she would be staying for the next week.

"Not too shabby, eh?" Cubie said as they entered the large and brightly lit room.

"Oh, wow," Therese said, looking all around her.

So unlike the Underworld, this first room opened up to the brilliant sky, and the light poured in and reflected on the golden walls trimmed with white molding. The furniture was upholstered in sky blue damask and cream silk pillows. A round table made of glass and gold was in the center and topped with a round crystal vase filled with cream-colored roses.

"It's so good to be home!" Galin exclaimed as she made herself comfortable in a ball on one of the chairs.

So Galin considered Mount Olympus her home and the Underworld her prison and not the other way around, Therese thought.

"Your room is through here." Hecate crossed the plush cream rug and white marble floor to a golden hallway that led to several other rooms.

Therese hadn't realized she would have her own private room, or that it would be as lavish as the main one. The golden walls and white moldings matched those of the first chamber, as did the sky-blue duvet and cream silk pillows on the bed. A gold and glass vanity and matching wardrobe were situated on the back wall beside a door leading to a private bath. It was just as luxurious.

"This is amazing," Therese said as she put down her bags.

Hecate winked. "You might not want to go back."

***

Hip was filled with agony as he watched Jen gaze into the dream globe and call his name. How had he managed to make her life worse than it had been before she had met him? He wished he had the power to turn back time and omit the information he had shared with Pete about seers and their powers. Why hadn't he realized the temptation to play god would be too great for any mortal?

"Hip?" Jen's sweet voice called.

As he disintegrated and raced through the Dreamworld in a thousand different directions, he tried to shut out her desperate voice that stood out above all others praying to him that night. Gods and mortals lived different lives. They were too unlike one another to live happily together. No relationship between a god and a mortal had ever ended well. Why should this one be any different? He balled his fists and clenched his teeth and willed himself to forget Jen Holt. She was better off without him.

"Hip, where are you?" she called again.

The god of sleep held back his tears and ignored her.

***

Than had never liked the spring. His mother always left, leaving his father in a perpetual bad mood. As much as his mother loved his grandmother, he knew Persephone was unhappy being away from home for half the year. Plus, the Underworld was quiet without Hecate and her familiars. But this spring day was worse than any other because Therese had left for a week, giving him a small taste of his father's heartache.

He sat on the new sofa with Clifford curled beside him and stared at the blazing fire beneath the mantle.

*So far so good?* he prayed to Therese. He tried not to let her know how badly he missed her. It wouldn't help her mission.

*Yes,* she replied. *I've unpacked my things and am eating with Aphrodite and her Graces.*

*Have you asked her yet?*

*No. I'm waiting for the right moment. Aphrodite still hasn't been exactly warm toward me.*

*Where's my mother?*

*She's with Hecate and Demeter in the great hall visiting with Zeus and Hera and the others.*

*Ah. They're the diversion.*

*Exactly.*

He should let her get on with her work, so he stopped himself from saying anything more to her. She would let him know when she had something to report.

*I miss you,* she said, and his heart leapt.

***

Therese lifted the golden goblet and took another sip of wine. As awkward as she felt sitting among these other goddesses who may or may not like her or be trustworthy, she had to ask them. She cleared her throat.

"Aphrodite, there's something important I need to ask you."

Aphrodite's brows shot up with surprise and she gave Therese a look of warning. "Of course," she said, uneasily. "You may ask me anything, for we are fortunate enough to always have the strength of Zeus with us, everywhere we go."

Therese felt blood rush to her face. Aphrodite was warning her to be careful. Zeus was listening, and perhaps even watching them. It could be an attempt to win Therese's trust. Maybe Aphrodite was a spy pretending to be sympathetic, but that was too hard for Therese to believe.

"I was hoping you and your Graces would honor me by being in my wedding party, as my matron of honor and bridesmaids."

Tears sprang to Aphrodite's eyes. She stood from the table and embraced Therese. "I don't deserve it," she muttered, "but I am happy to do it."

Cinny's blue eyes crinkled with her wide smile, and she clapped her hands. Despite her high-pitched, child-like voice, she was one of the older Graces, about Algaea's age, though by human standards she seemed no more than thirty. "This will be the best wedding ever!"

"I will be sure to make it so," Thalia added. "First, I need to know your favorite kind of flower. Then, I need to know what colors you like. Oh, this will be beautiful!"

Thalia looked young, like Pasithea—barley twenty, but her matter-of-fact, take-charge voice made her seem older.

"I can't wait!" Cinny chimed in, clapping her hands once more.

As Aphrodite returned to her seat, Algaea asked, "Perhaps while you're here, I can show you a few different arrangements for your hair."

Aphrodite squeezed Algaea's hand. "She has a talent with hair."

"I'd love that," Therese said.

She liked Algaea best of the Graces, though Thalia was a close second. Euphrosyne, whom everyone called Cinny for short, was sweet but a bit too bubbly for Therese's taste. Maybe it was Therese's nervous anxiety over whom she could and could not trust that made Cinny's extreme cheerfulness rub her the wrong way. Under different circumstances, Cinny might seem less annoying. And although Pasithea was the opposite of Cinny in that she remained placid at every turn, it was a bit unnerving to Therese. She had a feeling Pasithea didn't like her and suspected it had something to do with Jen's relationship with Hip.

"Persephone suggested we have a spa day together in Poseidon's beautiful tub," Therese said. "Hecate got his permission."

"Oh, I've always wanted to bathe in his tub!" Cinny exclaimed. "I've heard that the salt water is particularly good for one's complexion."

"It has calming properties," Pasithea said. "That's what I've heard, anyway."

"I think you're right," Therese said. "It helped me a few years ago, that's for sure."

"So you've already bathed there once before?" Algaea asked.

"It was a terrible night," Aphrodite explained. "I told you about it, remember? She had to fight…"

"Oh, yes," Algaea said, her face flushing. "How brave you were."

Therese didn't want to talk about it. "Can we meet there tomorrow, then?"

"Sounds lovely," Aphrodite said. "If my father will allow it."

After their meal, Aphrodite invited Therese to her rooms, where Algaea experimented with Therese's hair. Therese sat before an enormous vanity made of white marble and sterling silver. A crystal chandelier hung above them from a white dome ceiling trimmed with silver moldings. A row of diamond-shaped windows about the size of dinner plates lined the ceiling near the top through which rays of sunshine spilled into the room.

Aphrodite, who had left earlier, now returned to comment on the newest style Algaea had fashioned for Therese's hair.

"I like it up," Aphrodite said. "It shows off her swan-like neck and becomes her dimpled cheeks."

Therese blushed, unused to such compliments.

Aphrodite stretched out on the chaise lounge behind the vanity and met Therese's eyes in the mirror. Thalia and Cinny sat together on the sofa across from Aphrodite discussing flower arrangements and ribbons. They had spools of ribbon in their laps and on the crystal table between them, and their animated chatter filled the room. Pasithea was no longer among them.

"So, tell me, Therese," Aphrodite said in a straightforward voice that held a conspiratorial tone. "Tell me, now that we're alone in my room where my father can no longer hear us. Is Athena planning something against my father?"

Therese was taken aback. "What?" She didn't know what to say. What if Zeus had put Aphrodite up to this? And why would she blatantly warn Therese in the dining hall only to interrogate her here?

"You can tell me," Aphrodite said with a strange smile. "I feel sorry for my sister."

Therese looked at the reflection of Algaea, which had turned ghostly white, and then of Aphrodite, unsure of what to say.

"I don't know of Athena's plans," she finally said. "What do you mean?"

"I heard her speaking with someone," Aphrodite said. "It may have been Apollo. Do they mean to overthrow our king? And, if so, who's involved? Hephaestus? Hermes?"

"Please, Aphrodite," Therese said with a dry mouth, trying to hide her trembling hands. "Don't talk to me this way. I know of nothing like that."

Aphrodite slid to the edge of the chaise and leaned forward. "Are you quite certain, Therese?"

"Quite."

"Persephone indicated there might be something afoot, maybe in conjunction with your wedding," Aphrodite prodded.

*Did you say something to Aphrodite?* Therese directed to the queen of the Underworld.

*No,* came Persephone's response.

*She claims otherwise. She's interrogating me now.*

*Say nothing. Zeus is no longer in the great hall.*

"Then maybe you should talk to her," Therese said. "Like I said, I don't know anything about it."

Therese avoided Aphrodite's company that evening and the following morning, sure that the goddess of love was working for Zeus. Instead, she visited with Hecate and her familiars and then strolled over to the stables to see Pegasus and the other animals. Cupid appeared and said hello, but he seemed suspicious, so she left not long after. She was saddened by the thought that his blood ran through hers and had given her great talent with the bow, and yet, they could not trust one another. When the time came for the spa day with Aphrodite and her Graces, Therese was more than a little afraid.

Fortunately, Persephone would be joining them while Hecate and Artemis kept company with Zeus and Hera. Therese felt less terrified with a known ally at her side.

***

Jen turned out Hershey and then went back to the barn. She was exhausted and wondered if her mother would break down and hire a hand for the spring, just until Pete was back on his feet. The medication may have calmed him, but it was also making him loopy and lazy.

She was putting away the tack when Bobby came in. Their mother was still out on Ace.

"Hey," she said.

"Hey. I'm glad we're alone." Bobby shoved his gloves in his pockets and warmed his hands at his mouth. "Hawh." He exhaled against his hands again and again. "My gloves are crap."

"What's up?" Jen asked. Bobby was never glad to be alone with her—though she wondered if they were really alone, or if their father's ghost was with them in the barn.

He tucked his hands beneath his armpits. "You know I've never been one to believe in ghosts and stuff, right?"

"Yeah?" Where exactly was he going with this? Jen stiffened.

"Well, Pete's got me thinkin'. What if he's right? What if Dad is trying to warn him?"

"What if he is?" Jen scrutinized her brother's face.

"I had a bad dream last night." Bobby turned his back to her as he fiddled with a piece of wire. "Dad told me to tell you that you were in danger."

Jen couldn't breathe. She locked her knees and nearly fainted. Reaching out for a post, she regained her balance but felt like throwing up. "Dreams are sometimes lies."

"It felt real," Bobby said. "I don't think you should go to Therese's wedding. I think something bad is going to happen there."

He turned to face her, his expression grim.

"Are, are you going?" she stammered.

"We can't all pretend to be sick," he said. "And I'm not the one in danger."

"Is that what you want me to do? Pretend to be sick?"

Bobby nodded. "I think Pete will feel better, too. I think worrying about you is what's put him off kilter, you know?"

She wanted to puke. Pete had always looked out for her, and here he was, doing it again, even though it was making him ill.

"Well, think about it," Bobby said just before he left her alone in the barn.

Jen sat on a stack of hay and tried to slow the beating of her heart. If only Hip would answer her prayers and help her through all of this, but he must be busy with some god trouble. She hoped he wasn't tied to a mountaintop again. Believing she saw a snake in the hay on the ground, she flinched. It was a piece of rope. She covered her pounding heart with a hand and fought to catch her breath.

"Oh, Hip," she whispered, still breathless. "Where are you?"

***

Although Therese had worn her bathing suit beneath her white silk robe, the other goddesses undressed with ease before each other in Poseidon's luxurious bathroom behind closed doors. Not wishing to be teased about her modesty, Therese slipped off the yellow bikini and climbed into the swirling hot salt water with the others. The only things left on her body were her two lockets, which she never removed.

Aphrodite seemed different today—less sure of herself. She hadn't said much to Therese since the interrogation the day before, but now as they all closed their eyes and tried to relax in the calming heat of the tub with candlelight bouncing against the clamshell mirror and turquoise walls, she reached out and took Therese by the hand.

Well, that was different, Therese thought, but she wasn't about to pull her hand away from the goddess of love, no matter how awkward she felt.

Pasithea, who sat in the water on the opposite side of Aphrodite from Therese, flushed with jealousy and took her mistress by the other hand.

Aphrodite turned to her with surprise, and then gave her a patient smile. "Dear Pasithea, will you please go and get my favorite mineral oil? I left it in my room by mistake."

Pasithea tried to hide her frown as she stepped from the tub, slipped on her robe, and left to run her mistress's errand.

Persephone, who sat opposite Therese from Aphrodite, gave Therese a reassuring smile.

*Try not to look so frightened*, Persephone prayed.

Thalia and Cinny had laid their heads back and were humming in harmony with one another. Algaea massaged the back of her neck and had closed her eyes.

As Therese was about to reply to Persephone, she was alarmed when Aphrodite suddenly pulled her under the water's surface. Therese sputtered, having accidentally inhaled a little of the hot, salty water.

"Listen to me, Therese," Aphrodite said. "Zeus appeared to you as *me* yesterday, when Algaea was styling your hair. He trapped me in his room and wouldn't let me out until later."

Therese's mouth fell open.

"Don't say anything you don't want him to overhear," Aphrodite warned, "even when you think it's me asking you. He wanted to be in my place here, but Hera would not allow it. He's listening above, but I don't think he can hear us under Poseidon's protected waters."

"Aphrodite, are you okay? Do you need to be rescued?" Therese asked, her mind reeling. She still wasn't sure what to believe.

"He's got me blocked. I can't hear anyone's prayers, not even those of my people! I'm his prisoner out in the open. I'm miserable!"

Therese believed the goddess of love, but she dared not speak her mind out loud. "What should I do?"

"Tell Lord Hades."

At that moment, the others submerged, too, and looked at the two goddesses with curiosity. Aphrodite smiled at them and said something about the effects of the salt water on their complexions, so they all remained beneath the surface until Pasithea retuned with the mineral oil.

## CHAPTER THIRTEEN

# Dreams and Vows

In early April, Therese returned to the Underworld, after a visit to Colorado over her birthday weekend, where she had a fitting with the seamstress hired to alter her mother's wedding dress. Jen and Carol had gone with her. Therese had planned to break the news to Jen about Aphrodite's new role as matron of honor, but the time had never felt right. Jen had seemed depressed, and Therese hadn't wanted to add to her friend's poor disposition.

She had also gone to see Pete, and even in his medicated state—which had been eerily calm—he'd tried to convince her not to go through with her wedding.

If it hadn't been for the three precious evenings she spent with Lynn and her aunt and uncle, her birthday trip would have been an utter failure.

Back in the Underworld, Therese made her way through the winding chambers to the fields of poppy outside of Hip's abode. When she discovered he wasn't in his rooms, she stretched down on the cold flowers and went directly to sleep. She could have communicated with him through prayer, but what she had to say to him deserved to be spoken face to face, even if it had to be in the Dreamworld.

Gasping, she woke up in the world of dreams underwater, causing her to panic, like she had as an invalid at Poseidon's palace. She expected to see her parents in front of her drowning, dying. Terrified, she looked for them before she remembered that this was a dream and she had entered it with a purpose.

She swam through the water, no longer fearful. In fact, she enjoyed herself as she performed her favorite stroke—the breaststroke—at an easy pace. She willed a huge sea turtle to appear beside her, and he winked at her. Smiling, she returned the wink and took one of his flippers in her hand, which made her feel less angry and more relaxed. This would be better for Hip, for she had come here wanting to punch his face, and now she felt she was capable of a civilized conversation.

"Hip!" she called through the water. "Hip, I need to speak with you! It's important!"

He appeared before her in his blue trousers, but his usual white shirt was gone. Blushing, she hoped she hadn't been the cause of that like she had the very first time she had met him, while in the coma after her parents' murder.

"What's up?" he asked. Then, noticing the giant sea turtle, he added, "Cool."

"What is wrong with you?" she demanded. "Don't you know you can't tell a girl you love her and then one day stop speaking to her, with no explanation?"

He hung his head.

"How could you use my best friend like that?"

He glowered at her. "I didn't use her."

Therese let go of the turtle's flipper and crossed her arms. Of course, he would say that.

"Look, can we talk somewhere else? I'm not fond of the water."

Therese imagined a sunny, private beach covered in white sand. She and Hip walked side by side along the shoreline. "Better?"

"I'd forgotten how good you are at manipulating your dreams."

She was impressed with herself, too. She didn't visit the Dreamworld often anymore, and she'd forgotten how much she enjoyed controlling her dreams.

"What's going on? And don't say it's none of my business. She's my best friend, and I have a right to know, especially since you're a god and she's only human. I feel like I need to stand up for her."

A few seagulls cried out above the sea, and below them, a pair of humpback whales waved at them with their tales.

"Did you do that?" Therese asked.

"I'm trying to calm you down."

"I *am* calm. You're just stalling." She stopped to watch the magnificent humpbacks and muttered, "And it's working."

A cool, refreshing breeze blew her hair back from her face and lifted her spirits. Oh, he was good. He was real good.

"So, talk," she said. "I'm waiting."

He stood beside her and gazed out to sea. "I left the relationship because I'm in love with her. I mean *really* in love with her." He shoved his fists in his trouser pockets. "I've never felt this way before."

She turned to him, moved and shocked. "Then why leave?"

"For her own good."

They were silent for a while as she thought about that. Was it better for Jen if Hip wasn't a part of her life?

"You're not interested in having her become like us?" she finally asked him.

"Think that proposition through to its inevitable end," Hip said. "I have a million times."

It didn't take her long. "Ares?"

"He barely tolerates you. I'm sure you haven't forgotten all that he did to you, and *still* attempts to do to you. Don't you think he's working with Zeus to keep your wedding from being consummated? You're not out of the water yet."

A quiver raced down Therese's spine.

"Do you think I want Jen in that kind of danger?" he asked.

Therese sighed. "No. And although I have no regrets, I don't want her in danger either." She turned and faced him. "But I think it needs to be her choice. I think you should tell her everything you just told me and let her decide."

***

Than stood up when Therese finally returned to their rooms.

"Everything okay?" he asked.

She took off her bow and quiver and moved to the couch. "Yeah." As she curled in the corner and he sat beside her, she told him about her talk with Hip.

"Well," he said, "I guess Hip and I have something in common tonight."

Her head jerked up and she sought his eyes, perplexed. "What do you mean?"

Than smiled and gave her a light kiss. "There's something I want to talk to you about, that's all. Nothing bad, really."

He wasn't sure how she'd take his proposition. He thought it was a good idea. He hoped she'd feel the same way.

She squared herself to him in the corner of the couch with her legs curled in front of her—knees bent and open, lower legs crossed, in what people once called "Indian style." She looked adorable, even with that look of apprehension on her face.

He licked his lips and cleared his throat. Now that he needed to say it, it didn't come so easily.

"What do you want to talk about?" she prompted gently.

"Our wedding vows," he blurted out.

She pinched her eyebrows together. Then she relaxed and smiled. "Not what I was expecting, but a pleasant surprise."

He let out a breath. "Since things will be dangerous and chaotic during our wedding ceremony, I want to tell my vows to you tonight, so you're sure to hear them, and so you can focus on just me and you and not Athena's plan and Zeus's threat. Okay?"

Tears glistened in Therese's eyes. He couldn't resist leaning in and kissing her.

She uncrossed her legs and moved her feet to the floor so she could maneuver closer to him. She felt soft and warm as he ran his hands down her arms and took her hands.

"Are you ready?" he asked her.

She nodded, and he noticed a tear had dripped to her cheek. He gently rubbed it away with his thumb.

"Before I met you," he said, his heart rate picking up speed, "my life was a chore and a duty. I was like Sisyphus with his rock, doing the same things over and over. Unlike Sisyphus, I had a sense of purpose, but that was all that drove me. I didn't know real happiness and joy until you came into my life."

Tears welled in Therese's eyes, and he took a shaky breath before continuing.

"You are my teacher. I learn from you every day. I've learned to be more compassionate, more grateful, and more aware of the Upperworld. I've learned to make friends outside of my immediate family. I've learned to feel more confident in myself and to see that I am as good as the gods on Mount Olympus, and as worthy of honor and respect as any of them."

She nodded, encouraging him along, in spite of the tears that now poured down her lovely face. Tears filled his own eyes as he went on.

"You are my connection to things," he said, feeling breathless now. His hands were shaking, because he'd never given such a speech to anyone, and he wanted this to be right, to be perfect. "You have made me feel connected to life and to the world in ways that I hadn't experienced before you. Even my relationships with my own family members have become stronger because of you. You inspire me to be curious about the Upperworld. I didn't know what chocolate and coffee and tea were before we met, because I never cared or paid attention to anything but my duties. You opened up a whole new world for me and have made me feel connected to it."

Therese's mouth had stretched into something between a smile and a frown, and it trembled as quiet sobs began to overwhelm her. He squeezed her hands.

"You are my equal," he said. "Except for my power of disintegration and maybe for my skills in night Frisbee." He laughed, and so did she. "You are my equal in serving others, in defending people and other gods, in taking action to overcome injustice, and in doing everything to ensure that goodness and right always come out ahead of badness and wrong. In many ways, you surpass me. I admire your compassion and aspire to love other beings as much and as hard as you do."

Her entire body quivered uncontrollably now. She looked like she was falling to pieces before his eyes. He took her face in his hands and gazed into her eyes, which were streaming with tears.

"You are my love. My one and only, deep and passionate and eternal love. I cherish you more than anything in existence. I promise to love you, hard and true, and to protect you and that love, and to foster it into something new every day. I promise to be the one you can count on forever, and I will spend eternity doing everything in my power to make you happy."

There. He'd finished. He let out a sigh of relief. But before he could tell her he was finished and ask her what she thought of his speech, she closed the distance between them and gave him a wet, intense, lingering kiss that left him breathless again.

***

Jen leaned against the fence. Sassy came up behind and nudged Jen's hand.

"I don't have any treats, girl," Jen said. She was exhausted. With Pete still sick and the trail riding season upon them, she'd been working double time. Plus, she hadn't been able to sleep.

That wasn't exactly true, she thought to herself as she caressed Sassy's face. Jen hadn't *wanted* to sleep. Hip hadn't communicated with her through the dream globe or in her dreams in over two months. A few times she dreamt of him only to discover they were figments. She used the saying Therese had taught her to command the figments to show themselves, and Hip would disappear only to be replaced by a giggling, flying, eel-like thing. It gave Jen the creeps.

Her mom approached, bringing Jen out of her reverie.

"You go on and eat lunch and rest," her mother said. "John's going to help out again today."

Mr. Stern had been hanging around the Holt place more and more. Although Jen had felt awkward around him at first, she'd been grateful lately for his help.

"Are you sure?" Jen asked.

"Yep. Now go on."

After a quick sandwich, Jen put on her bikini and crossed the road to the lake for a swim. She missed the days when she and Therese would spend hours swimming and sunbathing together over the summers. It didn't take long for those feelings of nostalgia to shift to missing Hip. No matter how much she missed him, now that Therese had confirmed that he was okay and not chained to a mountain peak, Jen refused to pray to him. She might feel desperate inside, but she would never allow him to see it.

***

Therese turned down the dark corridor toward her favorite bat cave to think. Than's vows had filled her with love, but they had also filled her with fear. Hearing him promise to spend eternity trying to make her happy made her really think hard about what eternity would be like for her if Zeus succeeded in separating them. An eternity away from Than would be worse than death.

She wondered if it was too late for the transformation to immortality to be reversed. If Zeus swallowed Therese, could he take away her immortality, so she could die a natural death? The idea of living for all eternity inside Zeus's gut and perhaps hearing but not seeing or touching or loving Than, terrified her.

She'd never see her parents, her aunt and uncle, her sister, her best friend. Would she be able to communicate with her parents? Had Athena been able to communicate with her mother?

To add to the fear was her doubt that she could come up with vows worthy of Than's. His were so beautiful and touching. What could she say that would be anywhere near the same level of awesomeness?

*This is important*, she said to herself. *These last few weeks may be our final days together. I want him to know how I feel.*

As Therese sat with slumped shoulders on a ledge of rock among the baby bats waiting for the return of their parents, Athena appeared.

"Athena?" Therese asked in surprise. "What are you doing here?"

"Hello, Therese," the goddess of wisdom said. "I came here to talk to you."

"Oh?" Therese wasn't sure whether she should stand or remain sitting. Since her knees suddenly felt shaky, she opted for the latter.

"It's difficult for me to be open with you about all I want to say." Athena glanced around the cave. "Especially in this abysmal place."

Therese's face flushed. She frequently forgot how much the gods of Olympus despised the Underworld, and it shocked her every time she was reminded of it. This bat cave was special to her, and Athena found it repulsive.

"But," Athena continued, "I want you to know how pleased I am with the way you have conducted yourself since you joined our ranks. You and Thanatos may have begun your lives together hated by the other gods—looked down upon as oath breakers and as love-sick fools— but you have proved yourselves worthy to be among us."

Therese climbed to her feet, utterly astounded by Athena's compliments.

"Your willingness to take risks and to make great personal sacrifice, Therese, has not gone unnoticed." In spite of the darkness, Athena's gray eyes shined as brightly beneath her helmet as the glow exuded by her godly form. "I owe you many thanks."

Therese clutched her locket—the one that hung lower of the two on her chest, the one from Athena—and said, "So do I. Owe you thanks."

Athena lifted her brows above her dazzling eyes.

"After meeting Thanatos, I have received many magical gifts from the gods, but the words inscribed on this locket have helped me more than any other."

"Indeed. Words are the most powerful tools of all," Athena said just before she disappeared.

***

Hip had been searching for Jen through both the dream globe and the Dreamworld ever since Therese had confronted him, and that had been two days ago. How had Jen managed to stay awake for forty-eight hours, and why would she do it?

After several more hours, he sensed her as she sunbathed on the banks of the Lemon Reservoir across from her home. She was entering his realm, and he was waiting for her.

## CHAPTER FOURTEEN

# A June Wedding

The day before the summer solstice, Therese couldn't stand it anymore. She still hadn't shared her vows with Than, and this was eating her up inside. His speech to her had been so perfect. So beautiful. After trying for weeks to think of what to say and fearing she would never have another chance to say it, Therese stormed into their room, where he was eating, and, in a tone that sounded angry—she couldn't help herself—she said, "I need to tell you something."

He stood up. "What…"

"Sit down."

He sat, looking up at her, lines of worry crossing his face.

"I haven't prepared anything. I tried—believe me. So, I'm just going to speak from the heart"—a heart that was pounding loudly in her ears as she fumbled for the right words. "My speech won't be as long or as eloquent as yours, but it will be just as heartfelt, just as honest and true." Now if she could only think of it. "You told me I am your teacher, your connection, your equal, and your eternal love. And that meant so much to me." A sob threatened to choke her into silence. "Well, you are all those things to me, too." Really? Come on, Therese. Be original. "And, and I would add one more thing." She grasped for ideas, and it actually took no time at all to find the right one. "You are my reason." She was so pleased with this, because it was absolutely how she felt. The words finally came. She was on a roll. "You are the reason I became a god and the reason I try so hard to be a good one. You are the reason I strive each day to be better than I was the day before. I admire you so much, and I want, more than anything, to be worthy of your love."

He stood up again. "But…"

"Just wait. I'm not finished."

He sat back down with a look of tenderness on his face that melted Therese's heart. When she spoke again, her words came gently, softly, and through quivering lips.

"So, my promise to you is to love you forever and to always strive to be deserving of you."

This time when he stood, she did not stop him. He stepped from the table and took her into his arms. He didn't say a word. Instead, he covered her lips with his and spoke to her from the heart in a different way.

*****

"Are you sure, honey?" Mrs. Holt asked her daughter. "That dress looks stunning on you, and Therese will be so disappointed."

Jen dropped onto her bed and fiddled with the golden satin sash. "You're only making me feel worse. I can't help that I'm sick."

Jen's mother shook her head. "You're right. I'm sorry, baby doll. Should I stay home with you, then?"

"No, that's okay." Jen glanced up at her mother, who looked better than she had in years—hair dyed to its original blond and face glowing with powder and lip gloss. Jen had a feeling Mr. Stern's recent attention had something to do with her mother's transformation. "Just be sure and tell Therese how sorry I am. At least she won't have to worry about her matron of honor sharing the spotlight with me."

After her mother left, Jen felt like such a coward. How had she allowed a dream to stop her from going to her best friend's wedding? Without changing from the maid of honor dress Therese had picked out for her to wear, Jen lay on top of her covers and decided it was okay to have a pity party for herself as long as no one else was around to see it.

She had told Hip she wanted to become a god, but now she worried she didn't have it in her. Had the tables been turned, Therese would have gone to Jen's wedding no matter what. Jen felt like the biggest fraidy cat that ever lived.

*I don't want to die. Not today, anyway.*

A soft rap came at her bedroom door. She sat up, wiping her eyes. She thought everyone had already gone.

"It's me, Pete," her brother said. "Can I come in?"

"Yeah." She wished she had waited to open the floodgates a little later.

Pete stepped inside and frowned. "Don't be scared. Everybody's going to do everything they can to protect you. You've got Therese, Than, Hip, and a whole bunch of gods looking out for you, not to mention me."

That last part made her laugh. She loved her brother, but, really, what could he do? She lifted her smile to him and thanked him, surprised by how he, like their mom, had cleaned up so good. The gray tux brought out the deep blue of his eyes. She wondered if Therese ever regretted not picking Pete over Than.

"I'm staying here," she said.

"Good."

"You sure it's the right thing to do?" She twisted the skirt of her dress in her hands.

"I'm sure. It's safer."

Jen nodded, tears threatening to well once more in her eyes.

"We're leaving now," he added. "But we'll see you soon. I'm coming home right after the ceremony."

He shocked her by leaning down and kissing her on the top of her head, which had the opposite effect than was probably intended. It scared the heck out of her.

*He must think I'm going to die.*

***

Thanatos walked across the screened porch and entered the house.

"I don't think you're allowed up there anymore," Richard said from the base of the stairs. He was dressed in a gray tux with long tails, similar in style to Than's. "It's considered bad luck to see your bride all decked out."

Mortals and their traditions, Than thought as he gave Richard a forced smile. "Oh. Well, people are arriving. Am I supposed to greet them without her?"

"No worries. That's what the ushers are for. Pete's already on it, and the other two should be arriving soon. Come on. Let's go make sure everything's running smoothly."

The two men stepped outside where the gravel pad and drive had been transformed into something beautiful by Aphrodite's Graces. The rows of white chairs were beginning to fill up with people, some of whom Than did not know, and with a few gods incognito. His parents, Demeter, Athena, and Hephaestus were seated in the front row on the groom side. Mrs. Holt, Mr. Stern, and Bobby sat a few rows back on the bride side.

"Than!"

Than turned to find Therese's good friends, Ray and Todd, walking up the gravel path.

"Hey, guys," he said with a smile.

"Long time no see," Ray said.

"Congratulations, man," Todd added, shaking his hand.

"Thanks."

They both wore gray tuxes and sunglasses in the bright, late-morning sun.

"Hey, boys," Richard said, behind Than. "Nice to see you. Thanks for coming. Are you ready to help usher the other guests? Some arrived a bit early, but Pete took care of them."

"Reporting for duty, sir," Ray said with a laugh.

As the ushers helped the guests—gods and mortals alike—fill up the chairs, Than kept a close eye on Zeus, who stood in vibrant gold robes beneath the floral arch, waiting, like a bird of prey. The king of the gods did not fidget or smile but stood still like a panther ready to strike.

*What are you planning?* Than wondered.

Soon Apollo and three muses arrived with violins and took their places near the floral arch, playing a variety of soothing melodies as the rest of the audience took their seats. Poseidon, Amphitrite, and two of their daughters sat just behind Than's parents next to Hephaestus's daughters. Hera, escorted by Ares and accompanied by Cupid, Deimos, Phobos, and Anteros, took the row behind them. Artemis, Callisto, and their entourage of nymphs arrived and were soon greeted by the three ushers, whose faces had all taken on a permanent hue of pink. They probably hadn't been around this much beauty ever before in their lives.

Than was pleased to see that Ariadne, who had threatened not to come if no god would transform her brother into human form for the wedding, had come anyway. Thank goodness, because no one in the Athena Alliance could figure out a way to change him, and Dionysus would not have been happy if Ariadne had not shown up. He had become a key player in their plan.

"Speak of the devil," Than murmured to himself as Dionysus strolled forward to take a seat beside Ariadne. Thankfully, he wore more clothes than was his usual custom.

Hestia then arrived with her maidens, followed by Dione, all whom the ushers had no choice but to seat on the bride's side. The seating on the groom side was completely full.

Some of Hermes's children began walking up the path toward the ushers, but the messenger god was not to be seen. This worried the god of death.

"Nervous?"

Than turned to see his brother smiling back at him.

"Yes, but not for the usual reasons, unfortunately," Than replied.

"Never fear," Hip said with a wink. "Your best man is here."

"And you say I'm corny?" Than grinned.

*According to Athena, everyone is ready,* Hip conveyed to Than through prayer. *We've got the greatest might on our side.*

Might didn't always win. Cleverness and trickery had a better track record.

With his hand on Than's shoulder, Hip guided him to stand beside Zeus beneath the floral arch. Zeus narrowed his eyes at Than, providing no pretense of this being a happy occasion. Anxiety hammered on every bone in Than's body. This was it. Everything was about to go very right or very wrong.

Todd now seated Carol, who held Lynn in her arms. When she and the little girl took their seats, Demeter moved beside them and gave Than a reassuring wink. Meg and Tizzie swept in late and sat in the very back just as Apollo and the muses began the wedding march. Than guessed it was Alecto's turn to mind the store.

Then the Graces emerged from the house wearing matching golden gowns and sparkling golden tiaras in their hair. One by one, they carried beautiful sprays of white calla lilies as they walked down the center aisle to take their places in the front. When Aphrodite appeared, also in gold, a collective gasp swept over the crowd. She was the most beautiful creature alive. In spite of that beauty, she could not eclipse the bride, at least not in Than's opinion, for when he saw Therese step down from the wooden deck on Richard's arm, she took his breath away, and for a moment, a *very brief* moment, he forgot the impending conflict around him

*You look incredible*, he prayed to her.

***

It suddenly occurred to Hip that the prophecy from Pete had said nothing about the person who was fated to die being present at the wedding. What if Jen were in worse danger alone at her house than she would have been here among the gods? More than anything, Hip wanted to god travel directly to her, but the witching hour was upon them, and he had to remain at his station.

***

Therese mustered a smile for Than, despite her nerves, as she held onto her uncle's arm. Her father hovered just above them, causing several people in the crowd to say, "Look at that red bird!" and "Wow, look at that!" and "It's a sign!"

Her mother, perched on one of the elms, tweeted, "Quit stealing the show, Gerry!"

Therese should have laughed, but instead, she was on full alert. She made note of everyone's position. It was almost time.

Zeus gave her a smug grin as she approached him.

*Are you okay?* Than asked as he took her hand.

She smiled at him and nodded.

"Dearly beloved," Zeus began in his deep, booming voice.

As Zeus delivered the traditional speech to the crowd, Therese cued Amphitrite, who cued her son-in-law Briareos, the storm god. Within seconds, a huge cloud drifted over them.

Zeus glanced at the cloud but did not hesitate in his speech. "Do you, Therese, take Thanatos to be your lawful wedded husband, to have and to hold from this day forward?"

"I do." No tears threatened to spill from her eyes like they had the night Than had shared his vows with her. Today she had no time for tears and sweet sentiments. She glanced back at Carol and Richard.

Richard mouthed, "Thanatos?"

She would have to explain later why Zeus hadn't called him Thancules—that is, if she weren't in the belly of Zeus.

"Thanatos," Zeus continued. "Do you take Therese to be your lawful wedded wife, to have and to hold from this day forward?"

"I do," Than said with a charming smile.

Who could have known he was better at acting than she?

At that moment, Briareos dropped a deluge upon the wedding. Therese shot into the sky to the east with her bow and arrows, and, once above Quebec, took aim and shot each of the Cylopes as they gazed upon their thunderbolt-laden sheep. She should have been trembling with fear, but she was steady with determination. This was the most important battle of her life. In an instant, Therese rushed back to the ceremony to help usher the mortals onto the deck and under cover from the rain.

At the same time, Poseidon and Hades leapt forward and pinned each of Zeus's arms as Persephone and Hephaestus bound him with an iron chain. When Zeus gave the command for his thunderbolts, nothing happened. Hermes appeared, red-faced.

"The Cyclopes refuse to cooperate!" Hermes cried. "And they won't let me near the sheep!"

Therese had no time to glow with victory, for, from that moment on, everything was a whirlwind. Athena and Artemis captured Hera. Dionysus and Apollo overpowered Ares. Aphrodite demobilized Hestia. Dione bound her grandchildren with Amphitrite's help. God fought god, and all seemed to be going according to plan until Therese noticed Jen scurrying up the gravel path beneath her polka-dotted umbrella.

***

Jen couldn't stand herself anymore. What a coward. This was one of the most important days in her best friend's life. How could she not be there? She glanced at the clock on her nightstand. It was ten-fifty-seven. She had three minutes to get herself there before the ceremony began.

She thrust her feet into the gold satin pumps, snatched up her purse, and headed to her truck in the garage. When she backed out, she was surprised to see a giant thundercloud looming in the sky. Turning up the road toward Therese's house, she hoped and prayed the rain would wait until after the ceremony.

***

As soon as the wedding guests were seated at the tables on the covered deck, Hypnos embraced his role as god of sleep and, in his presence, every mortal fell asleep. Some lay their heads on the linen-covered tables. Others leaned back, mouths opened, and snored. Still others dropped against another person, and a few slipped from their chairs to the wooden floor.

Immediately, Hip disintegrated into the hundreds, dispatching one of his selves to the Holt place to check on Jen. When he saw her driving over to the wedding, he let out a curse. If she'd been home, he could have put her in the deep boon of sleep and carried her away. If he appeared to her now, as she was driving, he'd risk causing a crash. He'd have to wait to approach her when she was safely out of the vehicle and sleep could not harm her.

To his surprise, Pete bolted up from a table and stood facing him, fully awake.

"Hypnos, listen to me." It was the voice of Cybele. "Zeus plans to take your mortal girlfriend."

"But he's bound. He's no longer a threat," Hip said, even though he was surrounded by chaos as god fought god.

Pete seemed to become aware of what was happening, for it was his voice that cried, "Where's Jen?"

Just then, Jen parked her truck on the gravel path. She had taken several steps beneath her polka-dotted umbrella when Hip rushed to her side, and she fell asleep in his arms.

Pete marched down the wooden steps toward them. "Get her out of here!"

Before Hip could stop it from happening, Hermes's spear, meant for Hip, struck Pete's back, and the seer fell, face first, onto the ground.

"No!" All one hundred incarnations of Hypnos screamed through the pouring rain. Not Pete! Jen's heart would never be the same if her brother died.

Hermes was clearly mortified by what he had done. He gawked at Hip as he hovered above him.

Hip disintegrated into another ten and attacked Hermes, binding him with more of the iron chain Hephaestus had wielded specifically for this day. Jen lay asleep in his arms as another of him tended to Pete. But it was too late. The seer was dead.

## CHAPTER FIFTEEN

# The Prisoners

When Therese saw Hecate arrive to take Pete's soul, she picked up the skirt of her wedding gown and rushed from the wooden deck to the gravel path. Hip knelt on the ground beside Pete's body and, in a second form, held the sleeping Jen in his arms.

"No!" Hip cried again. "The spear was meant for me!"

"Please, Hecate!" Therese said. "Don't take him to the Underworld! Maybe we can put his soul into an animal, like we did my parents! I can make him immortal!"

Than appeared beside Therese and took her in his arms. "We can't keep doing that with every mortal you love. Besides, Pete might not want immortality. We can't make that kind of choice for him."

"Don't let this happen, Than!" Therese begged. "This is too much! Mrs. Holt won't be able to take it! This will kill her!"

"Go on, Hecate," Than instructed. "His soul becomes more vulnerable to abduction the longer you wait."

"I'm sorry," Hip said to Therese.

"But Melinoe's in Tartarus!" Therese insisted.

"There are others," Than said.

"Are you still jealous of Pete? Is that why you won't help me?" He couldn't possibly feel threatened by Pete, could he? But why else would he hesitate to help her?

"What?" Than's face turned white.

She immediately regretted her words. How stupid of her to say such a thing. She was just upset. Not thinking. "I'm sorry, I…"

Therese couldn't breathe as she looked around in desperation and noticed that the rain had stopped and all of the gods, save Than and Hip, were gone. Only the sleeping mortals remained. The Athena Alliance had taken their prisoners to the Underworld, as planned. Therese should be pleased that their mission was a success, but, instead, her heart was breaking for the Holt family and for herself. She had loved Pete. He was her friend.

*Poor Pete!*

"How can we explain to the mortals what happened?" Therese asked as the tears ran down her cheeks.

"We'll blame it on the storm," Than said. "Pete was struck by lightning."

She wondered if the mortals would believe it when there hadn't been a single streak of lightning or bolt of thunder in the sky. She had seen to that with her arrows on Cyclopes Island.

Than lay Pete on the drive. Therese turned away from the sight and followed Hip as he carried Jen into the house and stretched her across the couch. Tears poured from Therese's eyes as she watched him tenderly caress her best friend's hair and face.

"She'll never forgive me for this," Hip said.

"It wasn't your fault." Therese took Jen's hand in hers.

"She won't see it that way." He leaned down and kissed Jen's lips as though he were doing it for the last time.

Therese suspected Hip was right. Jen could be stubborn and pigheaded, and it would take her a long time to get past the death of her brother. Jen would blame Therese, too.

Than walked in. "Are we ready?"

He was referring to their plan to recover the mortals in the wake of the conflict.

Therese glanced at Hip, who nodded.

A few of the gods from the Athena Alliance had returned, ready to do their part. Amphitrite signaled her son-in-law, Briareos. The downpour returned, Hip vanished, and the mortals awakened, confused.

"What a storm!" Than shouted.

The mortals glanced around as Amphitrite, her two daughters, and Dione rushed under the deck to give the impression that no time had passed since the first downpour. Then the two Furies hastened up the steps, Tizzie exclaiming, "Where did that come from?"

Carol scrambled over to Therese and put her hand on the bride's shoulder. "I'm so sorry your wedding was ruined! That storm came out of nowhere!"

"It's okay." Therese gave Carol a forced smile and then exchanged a sad look with Than.

Richard came up behind them. "I didn't get to hear whether your uncle finished the ceremony. Did he pronounce you husband and wife? Where is he, anyway? Are you two actually married?"

Therese was at a loss for words. The death of Pete, combined with coming down from the intense rush of battle, had her feeling exhausted and defeated.

"Yes," Than said. "Therese and I are finally married."

Her eyebrows shot up of their own accord. Were she and Than indeed married, or was Than simply appeasing the mortals?

"Congratulations!" Carol cried, moving in to embrace them.

Others made their way over to Therese and Than to congratulate the couple as the rain began to dissipate. That's when Bobby noticed Pete lying on the gravel path.

"Pete!" Bobby cried in the voice of a much younger, frightened child.

"Pete?" Mrs. Holt screamed, maneuvering down the wooden steps.

Therese covered her stomach, about to be sick.

***

Hip followed Hecate as she escorted Pete's soul to Charon's raft and down the winding river through the gates of the Underworld. Cerberus uttered his usual growl as the gates opened, and then together, the passengers rode inside. The river took them straight to the three judges. Although Hip was expecting the sentence that was given, he nevertheless gasped when the judges pointed the raft in the direction of Tartarus.

He'd never seen anyone condemned firsthand. It was a humbling experience if not a frightening one.

"What's happening to me?" Pete asked.

Charon said nothing but continued to move his long pole through the dark water as they travelled through the misty tunnel toward the pit.

"Your soul is moving on," Hecate said gently, her hand on his ethereal shoulder.

"What? You mean I'm dead?" Pete's face twisted in terror.

Hip wished Pete could be dipped into the Lethe. It would make his transition so much easier. But souls destined for Tartarus were not permitted the gift of forgetfulness.

"It's okay, Pete," Hip said. "You should be proud of yourself. You saved Jen's life."

Pete's face transformed from a look of terror to one of relief. "Thank God." Then he asked, "She's safe, right? The gods didn't kidnap her, did they?"

"She's safe," Hip replied, moved by Pete's profound love for his sister. This is how siblings should treat one another: not like his uncles and father. At that moment, he determined he would do everything in his power to convince his father to allow Jen a visit to see her brother.

He followed Hecate and Pete through the iron gates of Tartarus, past those poor souls who were being tormented by Alecto, and down the winding path into the region of the seers, where Tiresias was waiting for them.

"I was expecting you," the blind man said. "Welcome to hell."

***

Than did not want to part from Therese as she helped the mortals re-cover from the loss of Pete, but he couldn't leave his duties in Hecate's hands indefinitely, and the Athena Alliance needed him.

"What about your honeymoon?" Carol asked after Than had suggested that Therese stay in Colorado for a few days. The ambulance had just left with the Holts.

"That can wait," he said grimly. "It wouldn't be much of a celebration right now anyway."

"He's right," Therese said through tears. "I'm in no state for a honeymoon."

Even though he felt the same way, Than felt a stab of pain with Therese's words. He wished for once that being with him could be the most important thing in Therese's life, like it had been when they first met.

"Why don't you stay, too?" Carol asked. "Why do you have to go?"

Than had no answer. "Um…"

"Hip needs him," Therese said. "Hip considered Pete a good friend and is really upset."

That was fast thinking on Therese's part, and it was probably true.

"Oh." Carol didn't hide the surprise from her expression. "Alright then." Tears welled up again in her eyes. "I'm so sorry this happened on y'all's special day." She wrapped an arm around Therese and the other around Than.

Than patted Carol's shoulder and was grateful Therese had so many loving family members in her life. He was also glad that being with him hadn't meant complete separation from them. He just hoped there wouldn't be any more casualties. First Vicki and now Pete.

"Me, too," Therese said through thick sobs. "It's going to be hard to face the Holts."

"Go get changed, and we'll head over there," Richard said, meaning the hospital.

Than wondered if Therese regretted the choice she had made to join him. Maybe she was beginning to think the price had been too great. He kissed Carol's cheek and then Therese's.

"I'll see you soon," Than said to them. He shook Richard's hand.

A lump rose to his throat as he walked away from the house and god travelled to his own.

He found Hecate and took back his duties. One of him remained with Pete in Tartarus, hoping to help him adjust; but he also disintegrated and dispatched toward the Athena Alliance.

He sensed the prisoners being held in isolated chambers. The first one he came to held Hera, and she was being interrogated by Artemis and Persephone. Than hovered near the entrance to eavesdrop.

"Don't you see how he's abused you?" Artemis asked. "You used to be the most beautiful and gracious goddess of all of us. His indiscretions have made you pathetic and evil!"

"How dare you!" Hera growled.

Than believed Artemis spoke the truth. His Aunt Hera was once considered the most beautiful of all the gods, even more beautiful than Aphrodite.

"You bound him yourself once," Persephone added. "This is your chance to do so again and to negotiate for what you want."

Hera might be the one god who could convince Zeus to cooperate without further conflict.

"That's right," Artemis said. "You can make demands with the rest of us. Demands for change."

Than moved on without revealing himself, curious to hear what was going on in the other chambers. In the next room, he sensed Hermes, and with him were Apollo and Hip.

"This isn't about changing regimes," Apollo said. "We considered it, but ultimately decided we would rather reform our system than rebel against it."

"So, my father will remain king?" Hermes asked.

"If he agrees to certain conditions," Hip said.

Than hadn't expected Hip to speak to Hermes after the messenger god struck Pete. It had been an accident, but the spear had been meant for Hip. Yet his brother spoke to Hermes with civility rather than hostility. That was good, he supposed.

Anxious to find the room containing Zeus, Than moved on. He passed Hestia, who was being questioned by Meg and Hecate, and then, in another room, Ares, who was with Aphrodite and Hephaestus. Aphrodite pleaded with Ares to see the light, saying again and again, "Do it for me." The god of war did not reply.

Than hadn't walked much farther when he heard Poseidon's voice reverberating throughout the rocky corridors. Than followed it into one of the deeper chambers, his heart picking up speed, like a boy who stands before the lion's cage.

Athena said, "We don't want to overthrow you, Father. How can you get that through your thick head?"

"The head you plan to slice open," Zeus said.

"If you hadn't swallowed my mother, I wouldn't need to slice it open."

"Enough of this!" Poseidon shouted again. "I'm sick of this petty bantering. We are going to free Metis, like it or not. And we will not unbind you until you swear on the River Styx."

"I swear nothing," Zeus said calmly. "Except this: When I break free of these binds, Thanatos—yes, I sense you out there—when I break free, the very first thing I'm going to do is swallow your sweetheart."

CHAPTER SIXTEEN

# Freeing Metis

At the hospital, after the doctor had come and said there was nothing that could be done, Therese apologized over and over to Jen, but Jen clung to her mother and ignored Therese.

Therese couldn't say she blamed her.

Mrs. Holt, who sat between her two weeping children, kept saying, "It's not your fault, Therese. No one can control the weather."

Jen said nothing out loud, but through prayer, she said, *Stay away from me! All of you gods stay out of my life! If you hadn't married Than, Pete would be alive. He's dead because of you!*

Jen was right.

Therese and her aunt and uncle drove home, where Lynn had been staying with Richard's parents and brother, house guests for another few days. After a somber evening, everyone readied for bed. Therese offered her room to Richard's parents—her Nanna and Paw-Paw—but they insisted on sleeping in the basement. Richard's brother took the couch. Therese couldn't very well explain that she didn't need her bed—that she wouldn't be sleeping in it, but she resigned herself to their wishes and pretended to go to bed, too.

Up in her room, she opened her window to talk to her parents. She tried to explain to them what had happened—what had really happened.

"Oh, honey!" her mother chirped. "You're just trying to do what's best for everyone."

"You can't blame yourself," her father added. "This is so much bigger than you or Jen or Pete. This is about fairness and justice for all."

"Life isn't fair, though" Therese said. "Only death is."

"But as gods, it's your job to make it as fair as possible," her mother sang. "And that's what you were trying to do."

"But this was about Zeus treating goddesses fairly," Therese argued. "It had nothing to do with mortals. Maybe it was a mistake."

"If Zeus treats goddesses so poorly, then he can't think much of females in general," her father said.

"He's right," her mother said. "What you're doing is trying to protect the voice and power of females, whether they are immortal or not. It's the right thing to do."

"You have to act if you want change," her father added. "Change rarely happens on its own."

That was true, Therese thought. And this gave her an idea. "I've got to go."

"Where are you going?" her dad asked.

"To Tartarus. To see Pete."

Therese found Than sitting on a rock beside Pete, trying to explain. Not wanting to interrupt, she remained back in the shadows, though she was sure they could both sense her presence.

"Forever?" Pete asked. "I don't even have a chance at redemption?"

"Playing god is one of the unpardonable sins," Than explained. "But you won't be tormented like most of the souls in Tartarus. You'll have a quiet, peaceful life."

"Away from everyone I love."

"Not everyone," Therese said, stepping into view. "I'll come visit you every day. And when your mother dies, I'll bring her in here to see you whenever I can."

"She won't know him," Than said.

"No, but he'll know her."

"Hip got Hades to agree to one visit from Jen," Than said.

Therese arched a brow. "How did he manage that?"

"How else? He made a deal my father couldn't refuse. Hip didn't say what it was."

She wondered what Hip would have to do in exchange.

"I can see Jen?" Pete asked.

"I'm not sure when," Than said. "But hopefully, soon."

"I'm going to do everything I can to help you, Pete," Therese promised. "Everyone deserves redemption. No sin should be unpardonable."

Than's face changed into a grim expression. "What are you saying, Therese? Zeus now, and next my father?"

"If that's what it takes," she said, though she hoped it wouldn't come to that.

***

The gods of the Athena Alliance gathered around and watched with baited breath as Hephaestus raised the hatchet above the sleeping Zeus's head. Athena stood opposite him, ready to help her mother to be re-born. Than became vaguely aware of his balled fists and clenched jaw as he carefully watched the drama unfold.

So many things could go wrong. He held his breath and glanced at his father as the hatchet came down and blood spurted in one long spray before settling into a slow leak. Zeus awoke with a wail, and he glowered at Hephaestus and the others gathered around him from his chair where he remained bound. Than expected Metis to leap out and shout for joy at her liberation, but when she didn't, he wondered if she was ever really in there.

"Mother!" Athena shouted. "Mother, come out!"

Than stood ready to take Zeus's soul to await his body's rejuvenation. Than had never, in his history, had to escort the lord of the gods to Tartarus. He'd taken countless other gods, including Apollo, but never Zeus. Than admitted to himself that he was a little frightened, but he was ready. He wanted this to be over. He wanted to get back to Therese and begin their lives together as husband and wife. Yes, Than was ready, but the lord of the gods would not die.

Apollo dared to widen the opening in the side of Zeus's head. Still, nothing happened.

"Let's try the belly," Apollo said. "Hypnos, put Zeus back into the deep boon of sleep."

"Yes, please do," Poseidon murmured.

"Don't you dare!" Zeus shouted. "I want to be awake to witness your treachery against me!"

"As you wish," Apollo said.

He exposed the king's belly before taking a scalpel from his medical bag and slicing through the skin. More blood bubbled to the surface as Zeus grit his teeth. Than thought for sure Zeus's soul would detach, but it did not. It held on to its body with fervor.

"Mother? It's me, Athena! Please come out and see me!"

"Dear sister, please emerge!" Amphitrite cried from where she clung to Poseidon's arm.

"She's probably terrified," Persephone said gently. "She's been in there for centuries."

"You have nothing to fear," Hephaestus said. "You are surrounded by friends."

"Do you think she can hear us?" Dione asked.

Aphrodite held her mother's hand. "That's what I was wondering."

"Could she be asleep?" Meg wanted to know.

"Hypnos?" Hades asked.

"She's not asleep," Hip replied.

Artemis stepped forward and thrust her hand inside Zeus's belly. "I'll come in after you, if I must."

At that moment, Than thought Artemis to be the bravest of them all.

"Be my guest," Zeus, breathless, spat. "There's room for two of you in there."

"Hypnos, please put this bastard to sleep," Artemis said.

Than noticed Therese's face lose its color. Beads of sweat clung to her pretty forehead.

*Are you okay?* he asked her.

She looked his way and gave him a subtle nod.

"Should I put him to sleep?" Hip asked Hades.

"Do not defy me, Hypnos! I will make you regret it! You don't think I will take that mortal girl you fancy and ruin her even more than I have already?"

Than saw his brother pale.

"Do it," Hades said to Hip.

Hip then stepped forward and waved his hand over the lord of the gods.

Zeus's head drooped in the chair, his body held upright by chains.

"You can speak freely now, Metis," Artemis said, with her hand still inside Zeus's belly. The huntress narrowed her eyes before seeming to land on what she was searching for. "Aha." She yanked with great force, and the upper body of Metis emerged from Zeus.

Her gray eyes, as fair as her daughter's, looked upon the Athena Alliance with horror. "Let me be!" she cried in a raspy voice, unused to speaking. She looked down at Zeus's mangled body and gaped, despite the fact that her own black hair was soaked with blood and her skin was pale from no sunlight. "Lord Zeus?" She glared at the gods around her. "What have you done?"

Than was at a loss as to how this prisoner could be outraged by the treatment of her captor.

*Not what I was expecting,* Than prayed to Therese.

*No,* she agreed.

✳✳✳

"But, Mother," Athena said. "Don't you want to be with me?"

Like Than, Therese was befuddled by Metis's reaction to what was supposed to be her liberation.

Metis's eyes alighted upon her daughter. "Athena?"

"It's me, Mother." Athena stepped closer to Metis, who remained half in and half out of Zeus's body. "Won't you please come out and embrace me?"

Therese thought of how badly she had missed her own mother and of how happy she was to be reunited with her again. Therese had gone three years; for Athena, it had been centuries.

"Oh, my dear child!" Metis exclaimed. "I never believed I would ever look upon you with my own eyes again!"

Metis broke into sobs as Athena rushed to her and put her arms around her mother.

Hades and Poseidon both stepped forward and each took one of Metis's elbows in an effort to lift her from their brother's belly.

"No!" Metis shrieked. "Leave me!"

The two brothers—the god of the Underworld and the god of the sea—hesitated.

"Why would you not want to be free?" Artemis asked.

"Perhaps she's been a part of Zeus for too long," Hephaestus offered.

"He's my lord and king," Metis sputtered. "I, I love him. I can't betray him."

"She suffers from what is known as the Stockholm Syndrome," Apollo explained. "I've seen this many times. From feelings of terror and infantile helplessness, victims become grateful to their captors and develop a kind of love for them."

"It is a perverted love," Aphrodite said. "I do not like it."

"A survival mechanism," Hades surmised.

"Indeed," Apollo said.

"Are we leaving her in or taking her out?" Poseidon demanded to know. "Dear gods, let's do something already."

"Patience, brother," Hades said.

"I have none." With that, Poseidon eased Metis from his brother's body. "Come on out and face the world, mother of Athena!"

Therese flinched as Poseidon and Hades lifted Metis from Zeus. The goddess trembled and wept. Athena took a quilt and wrapped it around her mother before helping her to sit in a nearby chair.

"There, there," Athena whispered gently. "You will feel better soon."

Apollo immediately began working to heal Zeus's body. First, he sewed up his belly, and then he stitched up his head. The other gods in the Alliance looked on silently until Apollo was done. Then Persephone recommended that they leave Athena alone with her mother for a while.

Therese agreed that this was a good idea. She remembered how she had hoarded her parents' company when they returned to the Upperworld as ghosts, just after Zeus's attack on the Underworld. She couldn't get enough of their company. She could imagine that Athena needed even more time than Therese. Centuries stood between Athena and Metis.

As the gods began to depart, Aphrodite touched Therese's arm and whispered, "I'm so sorry your wedding was ruined."

Therese smiled at the goddess of love, glad to have her back on the same side. She'd missed Than's aunt and had felt so hurt by her snubs—which she now knew were caused by Zeus. Tears rushed to her eyes at Aphrodite's show of kindness.

"It was for a good cause," Therese replied.

"Maybe now you can spend some time with your love."

Therese glanced across the room at Than who seemed to be waiting for Zeus to die. There was still so much to do, but maybe Aphrodite was right.

"I hope so," Therese said before going to Than and linking her fingers with his.

***

Hypnos returned to Tartarus to visit Pete. He discovered Tizzie already there talking to the seer.

"I know you were only trying to help," Tizzie said fondly. "Unlike some, who want to display their power to intimidate others, you have a kind heart."

Hip wasn't used to hearing his fierce sister speak in reassuring compliments.

"So why am I here?" Pete asked.

Hypnos stepped inside. "It's my fault. I should never have explained to you what seers can do. I should have known the temptation would be too great."

"Don't blame yourself, Hip," Tizzie said, standing from her rock.

Okay, since when did Tizzie not cast blame where it clearly belonged?

"Tizzie, what's wrong with you?" Hip asked. He was beginning to worry that she might be an imposter.

"I don't blame you," Pete said. "I take responsibility for my actions."

Tizzie turned to Pete and cooed.

Cooed? What was going on here? Hip wondered.

"I really like that about you," Tizzie said. She took Pete's hand. "I have a feeling you and I are going to be great friends."

Pete stood. "I guess I'm ready for that tour, then."

"Tour?" Hip asked.

"I'm going to show him around Tartarus," Tizzie said. "Introduce him to people."

"Oh." Like that wasn't odd, he thought. Nope. Not at all.

## CHAPTER SEVENTEEN

# Escape

Therese followed Than back to their rooms where Clifford and Jewels greeted them.

"I have a question for you," Therese said to Than after she had spent a few minutes with her pets. "When you told Richard we were married, did you mean it? Are we really married? Because I don't recall Zeus making any pronouncements."

She held her breath as she waited for Than to answer.

"We said our vows before our family and friends and all the gods." Than circled his arms around her waist. "We don't need Zeus to pronounce anything to make it official, do we?"

She gazed into his eyes as joy spread through her. A lump rose to her throat. Her voice cracked when she said, "I guess not."

"So, my dear wife." Than traced her jaw with his index finger, and her entire body responded to the word, "wife." His blue eyes smoldered. "You still have a few hours before morning in Colorado."

A smile broke across her face as a little nervous shiver worked down her back and she took her cue. "Whatever shall we do?"

He gathered her up in his arms and carried her off to bed. As he crossed the threshold of their bedroom, her heart pounded against her ribs. Tonight was full of so many firsts: it was the first time Zeus had been successfully bound, the first time Athena had gazed upon her mother since the day she had sprung from Zeus's head, and it was the first time Therese and Than would spend the night as husband and wife.

***

Hypnos had just lain down on his feathery soft bed for the first time in weeks when he heard a shrill cry resound throughout the Underworld. He sprang from his bed and prayed to his father.

*Has something happened?*

*That was Hera,* Hades replied.

Hip god travelled to Hera's room to find her weeping.

*Zeus is gone!* Hades warned.

Hera glared up at Hip from her chains. "He left me behind!"

Hip disintegrated and dispatched to the chamber where Zeus had been chained to find several members of the Athena Alliance in shock. Metis was among them.

"I'm sorry," Metis said to Athena. "I did this. I thought he would take me with him."

Hip wondered if Metis's supposed wisdom had been corrupted inside Zeus's belly.

Than entered. "Hermes, Hestia, and Ares are gone, too."

Hades and Poseidon exploded in rage.

"What have you done?" Poseidon shouted to Metis. "Now we are all doomed!"

"Prepare for battle!" Hades commanded.

Athena stood before her mother. "Will you fight with us or against us?"

"I am with you, daughter," Metis said through tears. "Please forgive me and let me fight with you."

"Hera is with us, too!" Artemis cried as she entered. "When I told her that Zeus had left her behind but had freed his sons and sister, she swore an oath on the River Styx to serve the Athena Alliance!"

"Wonderful!" Athena cried.

"Free her!" Persephone said with glee.

"Why haven't the thunderbolts rained down upon us yet?" Dione wondered out loud.

"Because Zeus has gone after Therese," Apollo said, giving Than a sympathetic look.

Than stepped forward on trembling knees. He'd *never* been so frightened in his life. "We have to help her. He's going to swallow her."

***

Therese pulled the apple pies from the oven and set them on the granite countertop. Although her aunt and uncle had already taken food over to the Holts this morning—wedding food the Graces had prepared for nearly a hundred guests—Therese had wanted to do something special. She hadn't baked an apple pie since her parents were alive as mortals, but she hadn't forgotten how to do it, and she knew it was Jen's favorite dessert. Despite her sadness over Pete, she was full of joy as she hummed around the kitchen with what she supposed was the glow of a newlywed.

"That smells wonderful," Nanna Bradshaw said from across the room.

"Thanks, Nanna," Therese replied. "I made one for you and Paw-Paw, too."

Richard's mother smiled. "How nice of you."

"Girl, are we proud of you," Paw-Paw said from Richard's recliner. "After all the misfortune that's happened here, you're holding yourself together, and baking pies to boot. You are a strong girl, Therese, darling."

Therese removed the oven mitts and crossed the room to her adopted grandparents. "Thanks, Paw-Paw. I'm just thinking of my blessings."

"We are the ones who are blessed," Nanna said. "To have you and your sister in our lives. Ain't that right, Lynn? You a blessing!"

Lynn wriggled from Nanna's lap and tottered over to Therese. "Horsies, Terry. Lynn wanna see horsies."

A few minutes later, Therese carefully laid one of the pies on the passenger seat of the Lamborghini and then buckled Lynn into the backseat.

"Let's go see the horsies," Therese said cheerfully.

"Horsies!"

When Therese pulled into the gravel drive, she couldn't believe her eyes: Jen, Bobby, Mrs. Holt, and Mr. Stern were in the pen fitting some of the horses with tack. Were they really going to give their usual trail rides today, the day after Pete's death? They hadn't even had his funeral yet.

Therese and Lynn had barely climbed from the car when Jen's prayers came flying toward her like darts.

*I thought I asked you to stay away from me? Whatever you do, don't talk to me. I don't want to talk to you.*

Therese held Lynn's hand with one hand and the pie with the other as she made her way toward the pen.

"Well, howdy, Therese," Mrs. Holt said. "What have you got there? Your aunt already brought a ton of food from the wedding. Good stuff, too." Although her voice was pleasant, the dark rings around her swollen eyes made her face look like a skull.

"I baked you an apple pie," Therese said.

"Jen's favorite. Why don't you take that on inside and put it on the kitchen table for me?"

"Sure will. Can Lynn see the horses?"

"Horsies!"

"Come on over here, Lynn," Mrs. Holt said.

Therese let go of Lynn's hand and headed toward the house. She hadn't gotten very far when the sky above her darkened and a flash of lighting bolted toward her.

Therese looked up and dropped the pie.

***

Than disintegrated and dispatched to Colorado, warning Therese of Zeus's escape as he god travelled to her aunt and uncle's house. Back in the Underworld, he had just asked for the help of the others when Metis jumped up from her chair with a finger raised in the air.

"I have an idea!" Metis cried.

"What, Mother?"

"I know where Zeus has hidden Cybele. We can rescue her, and she can then help us to overpower Zeus."

Of course, Metis would know, Than thought. She'd been in Zeus's belly all this time and heard all that had transpired between Zeus and Cybele.

Poseidon leaned against his trident. "You think highly of her powers."

"She is more powerful than you know," Metis said.

"She didn't show it as my prisoner last year." Hades picked his beard doubtfully.

That was true, Than thought. Cybele had sat in this very room cuffed and helpless when she sought asylum from Zeus.

"That's because she wanted to gain your trust," Metis explained. "But I suspect you aren't aware of Cybele's alter ego."

Than narrowed his eyes and waited to hear what Metis had to say.

"Alter ego?" Artemis repeated.

"What do you mean?" Apollo asked.

Metis folded her arms across her chest. "None of you recognized her. I suppose I'm not surprised."

"Enough riddles!" Poseidon shouted. "Tell us who she is!"

Than was growing impatient, too.

"She's your mother," Metis said. "The mother of all the Olympian gods."

***

Therese leapt into the sky to dodge the thunderbolt, but another one was fast on the heels of the first. The edge of it grazed her foot and sent a numbing sensation through her leg. Before she could react, a sheep fell through the air. And then another. And another. They bleated with terror as they fell toward the ground below. Therese swooped down to catch them. Although she was afraid the contact would cause the thunderbolts to go off, she had to try. It was her job as goddess of animal companions to save the friendly sheep.

She caught each sheep by a leg and delivered them safely to a San Juan mountain peak before charging toward Cyclopes Island with her arrows of love.

*Zeus swore to swallow you*, Than warned. *I'm closing in on him, disintegrated into a massive army.*

*Wait! If he succeeds in striking even one of you with a direct hit, you'll fall from the sky! Retreat, Than! Please! I have another idea!*

*I can't afford to lose you, Therese!*

*I won't let him swallow me. Trust me!*

Therese turned herself into a beautiful eagle, and as soon as she was in sight of Zeus, who hovered over the island flinging sheep left and right, she struck him in the heart.

"Clever girl!" he shouted as he reached for another sheep. "You know how I love eagles. And now you've made me care too much for you to harm you. But that doesn't mean I won't get my revenge on the others!"

She returned to her normal form and sent an arsenal of arrows into his heart so that each time he reached for a sheep, he moved it aside and reached for another. Soon, he loved every animal on the island. And all of his thunderbolts were deep inside their bellies.

Although she had not been able to save every sheep, Therese felt relieved to see so many grazing along the hills of Cyclopes Island. A few others wandered the San Juan Mountains behind her aunt and uncle's home. Satisfied, she returned to the shape of an eagle and descended on a nearby mountain peak in Greenland to catch her breath and to alert the others of Zeus's whereabouts when, to her horror, Zeus transformed her from the eagle back into her normal form, and, by the look on his face, the love her arrow had inspired in him did not hold after the transformation. He lunged for her.

***

Hip, accompanied by Alecto and Apollo, followed Than in Apollo's chariot to Colorado to help his brother protect Therese from the clutches of Zeus, but he also disintegrated and flew in his father's chariot with other members of the Athena Alliance toward the belt of Orion, where Metis had told them Cybele hung.

Hypnos was still in shock over Cybele's identity. She was Rhea, the mother of all the Olympian gods. He had once heard rumors about it, but he'd never taken them seriously. According to Metis, after Rhea, the daughter of Earth and Sky (Gaia and Uranus), had saved Zeus from being swallowed by her husband, Kronos, Zeus had grown up hidden away in Mount Ida, where Cybele, or Rhea's, Curetes had protected him from notice. Hip recalled the dancing men of the mountain who had helped to save Than and Therese and Hecate's familiars. Once Zeus had reached manhood, he overthrew his father to become the supreme ruler of the gods. Not long after, he cast his mother aside and gave her no importance among the Olympians.

What a way to treat your mother, Hip thought.

Afraid that Zeus would imprison her, Rhea changed herself into a hermaphrodite and called herself Adgistis, not realizing Zeus would find a god of both sexes a threat to his power. Rhea eventually became Cybele after Dionysus set her up for castration.

Metis had discovered all of this last fall when Zeus had returned Athena and had captured Cybele. Cybele had hoped that by revealing herself as his mother, Zeus might have pity on her. But he did not.

Zeus had dangled his mother from the middle star of Orion's Belt.

Just the thought of treating his mother in such a way brought a bad taste to Hip's mouth. He shook it off and focused on their journey toward the clouds. The chariot jolted when it breached the ozone and Earth's atmosphere to enter outer space. Orion's foot reached above them, and his belt, though made of stars light years away, manifested itself in a single layer around the hunter's waist.

"There she is!" Persephone cried.

From the center of the belt, Cybele hung on an iron chain fastened around her torso. Her long purple gown covered her feet, and her arms were lifted over her head, her hands curled around the chain.

"At last!" the manly goddess called as tears poured down her cheeks from behind her blindfold.

CHAPTER EIGHTEEN

# Face Off

Before Therese could god travel from where she perched on the peak of Mont Forel in southern Greenland, Zeus bounded down from the floating Cyclopes Island and snatched her up in his mighty hands. She barely had time to blink before she was whisked away to Mount Olympus, where Hermes and Ares were waiting.

When she tried to pray to Than and the others, she realized Zeus had her blocked. She had no way of communicating with the Alliance. No way to call for help!

Why, oh why had she told Than to retreat and to trust her? Here she was about to be eaten. How could she spend eternity in the belly of another? How ironic that Metis was freed only to have her replaced with Therese.

"Chain her to my throne!" Zeus commanded his sons.

Instantly, they wielded chains and cuffed and shackled her onto the double golden seat. She gave Hermes her most pleading gaze and prayed to him to help her, but he ignored her.

*Don't let him swallow me!* she begged Hermes.

"You have been a thorn in my side from the moment Thanatos laid eyes on you!" Zeus bellowed. "You failed to avenge the murder of your parents, you failed the challenges issued to you by Hades, and you persuaded Thanatos to break his oath to make you one of us. I might have tolerated you in spite of those shortcomings had you not become one of the major instigators of the treason against me and my kingdom."

"But…"

Zeus pushed his palm toward her and glared at her, his nostrils flaring. "You don't get to speak, Therese, goddess of animal companions! Your time is up!"

"You can't silence me!" she shouted just before she transformed herself into an eagle and flew above her captors.

Zeus immediately transformed her back, and this went on several more times before Ares caught her in her human form and pierced her side with his sword. The pain burned in her side like a hot flame that couldn't be extinguished. Blood poured down her hip and leg and onto the marble floor of the great hall.

Therese was returned to the double throne and to her shackles. Feeling dizzy and light-headed, she struggled to find the words to express to Zeus how she felt.

"When I first visited this place, I adored you," she said, breathless from the loss of blood. "You are so beautiful, so charismatic, and so strong."

Zeus did not interfere with her speech, so she continued.

"Everyone loved you," she said. "Still loves you. The members of the Alliance don't want to replace you, but to have you agree to certain conditions. Can't you see?"

"I'm not unreasonable," he said. "You and your allies didn't have to resort to such treason against me!"

"And you were just," she added. "Or so you seemed. The way you treat females, well, it's wrong."

"I have been faithful to Hera for hundreds of years!" Zeus said defensively. He turned to his sons. "What am I doing? I owe this girl no explanation!" Then he towered over Therese, his face red with rage. "But, yes, I've acted impulsively in the past, and the consequences haunt me. I was in the process of trying to restore harmony to my house when you and your allies interfered."

Therese's blood continued to seep from her body. "But what about Cybele? How would you like to be imprisoned away from the ones you love for all eternity?" She thought of Pete as tears slipped from her eyes.

"She betrayed her king!" Zeus thundered.

"To save Athena!" Therese thundered back.

"Enough of this! Athena was never in danger!" Zeus pointed a commanding finger her way.

Therese did not back down. "And Melinoe?"

"Cut her up into pieces!" Zeus ordered Hermes and Ares. "She'll be easier to eat that way."

Zeus turned and walked away.

"Where are you going, lord Zeus?" Hermes asked.

"I've lost my appetite. I'm going to rescue Hera and spy on the others. Have the goddess of animal companions ready when I return."

Once Zeus had left, Therese searched the eyes of her captors with fear and anxiety. "Please," she begged. "Please don't do this."

Hermes stood on her left and Ares on her right. The two brothers seemed to be speaking silently to one another.

"You don't have to hide your words from me," Therese said.

"I will not cut her into pieces," Hermes said. "I love my father, but I cannot follow that order, Ares. And I cannot allow you to follow it either."

"You will betray our father and our king for this girl?" Ares asked. "You would fight me for her?"

"I would rather not fight you," Hermes said. "But Zeus is wrong in this. He's gone too far."

*Thank you, Hermes!* Therese prayed. *Thank you!*

Therese lifted her face to Ares, filled with a new hope. "You have always stood for a level playing field between enemies. Isn't that right? It's what made you try to weaken the US through the murder of my mother."

"So?" Ares glared at her. Unlike Hermes, he showed her little mercy.

"Wouldn't the god of war wish to see the females fight for their right to power?"

For a brief moment, Therese recognized a gleam of understanding in Ares's eyes.

"Before Zeus took me here," Therese continued. "Than told me Hera swore on the River Styx to support the Athena Alliance."

"Why should we believe you?" Ares demanded.

"Your mother didn't know Zeus planned to return for her," Therese said, feeling physically weaker by the minute despite her new resolve. "She thought she'd been abandoned. Even Hestia got out with you, so you can imagine…wait, where is Hestia?"

"She's probably in the kitchen cooking," Ares muttered.

"No," came Hestia's voice from the entrance to the dining room. "I'm not cooking. I'm waiting."

Therese wondered what the goddess of the hearth had in mind.

"For what?" Hermes asked.

"For you both to see how wrong Zeus is in this," Hestia said.

Therese's hopes soared.

"How you cannot cut up Therese and feed her to our king," Hestia continued. "How you cannot stand by while Cybele hangs above the earth banished from the rest of the world. Do you know who Cybele is?"

"The manly goddess," Ares said.

"Yes. And she's also my mother," Hestia said with tears welling in her eyes.

Therese's mouth fell open. Cybele was Rhea?

"I did not know it until recently. It was bad enough to watch my brother forsake someone I believed to be a traitor, but to stand idly by while he persecutes our mother... I cannot stand by any longer. And so, I'm waiting to act. Waiting for you to join me."

"I will not join you against my father," Ares said.

"Then cut her up as you've been told," Hestia said, causing Therese to cringe. "Because when you do, Death will come to her, and no fortress, not even Mount Olympus, can hold him from a soul who calls. Zeus has forgotten why our father, Kronos, swallowed my brothers and sisters and me whole. If the soul isn't trapped with the body, the body will be expunged eventually, and Therese will be free. So go ahead, Ares."

The god of war looked first at Therese and then at Hermes. Therese trembled uncontrollably. Even her teeth chattered. Would he really slice her up like stir fry?

"We shall not cut her," he said to Hestia. "Now fetch something for her wound."

"I am not your servant," Hestia said. "But for Therese's sake, I will obey."

Therese released the breath that had been frozen in her lungs, glad she would not have to endure the pain of being cut into bits. But the anxiety continued to mount within her as she wondered what would happen when Zeus returned.

***

Jen ran from the pen toward the house, found the dropped pie, ruined, on the grass, and looked up to the sky.

"What's happened?" her mother shouted from the pen. "Is Therese alright?"

"Hip?" Jen prayed, still looking up at the dark gray sky. Lightning flashed between the clouds and thunder shook the ground beneath her feet. "Please protect Therese." As angry as she was at her friend, and as much as she blamed her for Pete's death, she still loved her and didn't want anything bad to happen to her. "Hip, can you hear me?"

Jen looked down at the ruined pie as tears welled in her eyes. She didn't think she could handle any more loss. Her father, Pete, and now…"Hip! Please!"

Hip appeared before her, his blue eyes full of emotion, but she immediately knew he was not in his mortal form. Drowsiness crept up her body like hot bath water.

"Save Therese," she managed to say just before she fell asleep in his arms.

***

Hip carried Jen into her house and laid her on the couch. Next, he went to the other mortals, and he put them all into the deep boon of sleep, so they might not be confused by Therese's sudden disappearance. One by one, he took them into the Holt family room and made them comfortable. He then used his powers to restore the pie, so it wouldn't be a reminder to them of what had happened, and he placed it on the kitchen table. Before he left, he leaned over Jen once more and touched his lips to hers. He hoped she would call to him again.

Demeter appeared and said she would watch over the mortals while the war between the gods waged on. She did not want to be a part of the conflict, and someone needed to keep an eye on the earth and its inhabitants.

Back on his father's chariot, Hip helped the other gods of the Alliance to unfasten Cybele from Orion's belt. When she dropped into their arms, she breathed a heavy sigh and then begged Hypnos to help her sleep for a while. He did her bidding as Hades guided Swift and Sure back to the great chasm and into the Underworld. Then he carried Cybele into a large, comfortable room and laid her out on a feather bed. Metis flocked to Cybele's side and stooped to her knees.

"Your poor mother," Metis said to the Olympian gods gathered round the bed. "I am so sorry for my part in this." She covered her face and wept.

Hip was moved by the solemn looks on the faces of the gods around the bed.

Athena put her hand on Metis's shoulder. "Cybele was Zeus's prisoner for six months, but you, Mother, were in his belly for centuries. I think we can all forgive you for your loyalty to Zeus."

Hera pushed through the gods to her mother's side. "Is it really true? Is Cybele Rhea?"

"So it would seem," Hades said, moving closer to the bed.

Hip stepped back to make more room.

"Why would she not make herself known to us?" Poseidon said, standing opposite Hades.

"There was a time when women were revered in a place of honor," Metis said. "Our grandmother, Gaia, is the Earth itself and the mother of all things, and the first creator of life, but in his desire to overthrow the Titans, Zeus diminished the role of females and cast his own mother out of his kingdom. He drew lots with his brothers, but why weren't Demeter, Hestia, and Hera given kingdoms to rule?"

Hip had never thought of it that way. He wondered why.

Artemis raised her bow. "We will demand change. We will force Zeus to agree to share his rule with Hera."

"And Persephone should have an equal say in my dealings in the Underworld," Hades offered.

Hip noticed a smile creep onto his mother's face.

Poseidon looked across the room at Amphitrite. "My wife already rules the sea more than I."

Amphitrite grinned. "Indeed."

"But what of Hestia and Demeter?" Metis said. "They still have no kingdom to rule."

Back on Apollos's chariot, Hip returned through the chasm with Alecto and Apollo without having found any trace of Therese. They entered the chamber where all were gathered around Cybele.

"Any sign of her?" Hades asked.

"She was taken by Zeus," Apollo replied.

Than appeared beside Hip. "I followed them as far as Mount Olympus. I couldn't get inside."

Athena raised her spear. "We must storm the gates."

"And we must act now," Persephone added.

"Mount Olympus is impenetrable," Hephaestus said. "Zeus added reinforcements after your sons exposed its weakness."

Hera stood from where she had been kneeling beside the sleeping form of Cybele. "What Hephaestus says is true. Zeus put wards around the wall that are more powerful than I've ever seen."

"We can't give up," Than urged.

Hip had never seen his brother look more desperate.

"How dare you suggest we might," Hades retorted.

"Let's rally up every ally we can find," Athena said. "We'll show my father that we're a force to be reckoned with."

CHAPTER NINETEEN

# The Athena Alliance

Ares stood near the door to the great hall. "Zeus is on his way back. No one leaves. Understand?"

Phobos and Deimos appeared on each side of Ares with their arms crossed looking like barroom bouncers. They glared at Therese.

*We can overtake them,* Therese prayed to Hestia and Hermes. *We have a daughter of Rhea on our side.*

Hermes went to the side of Ares and said, "I stand with my father. I will not cut you up, but I will remain on my father's side for as long as I can."

Therese sought Hestia's eyes and found a weak smile on her lips. Without the help of Hermes, and with Therese in chains, they were doomed.

Then Zeus appeared and assessed the situation. He looked at Hestia with shock and pain playing havoc with his face muscles.

"My dear sister?" Zeus said gawking. "Do you betray me, too?"

So it was true about Hera. Therese had never seen such a look of sadness on Zeus's face.

"I love you more than anyone," Hestia said. "But what you're doing is wrong."

Zeus amazed Therese by bending down on his knees. "I'm only fighting for my kingdom, dearest. Do you want to see me fall?"

"None of us want that," Therese chimed in. "We want justice."

"Silence!" Zeus's face transformed from supplicating to threatening in less than a heartbeat. "There will be no justice for you!"

Therese shrank back. She could see he was determined to eat her. Sweat broke from her pores.

"But you are the lord of justice," Hestia said gently. "Are you not?"

"Justice is not for one's enemies," Zeus said. "So, tell me, darling sister, are you my friend or my enemy?"

Hestia's eyes were full of tears. "You leave me no choice."

"You have broken my heart." Zeus stood up and turned his back to her.

Hestia covered her face with her hands and fell to her knees. "As you have mine."

***

Apollo and Hip, Amphitrite and Artemis, Alecto and Meg, and Hecate and Hephaestus had left in teams to recruit more allies when Cupid appeared with two Graces where the remaining members of the Alliance gathered around Cybele's bed. Than observed an expression of worry on the faces of the new arrivals and braced himself for the worst. He knew they weren't a threat. His father wouldn't have let them in if they were there to attack.

Aphrodite stood from her chair and crossed the room to her son. Cinny and Algaea embraced their mistress as tears flowed down their cheeks.

"We couldn't get Pasithea or Thalia out," Cupid said. "We barely escaped ourselves before Zeus returned."

"Now no one can get in or out without Zeus's permission," Algaea added.

Athena crossed her arms. "I was afraid of this."

Than stepped forward. "Is Therese…"

"Still chained to Zeus's throne," Cupid replied.

Than dropped to a chair and held his stomach, which was tied in a million knots.

"And Hestia has taken her side," Algaea said.

Than looked up. "Against Zeus?"

The Graces nodded.

Cinny mopped her face with her sleeve. "Hermes refused to cut Therese into pieces. He even stood up to Zeus."

"But as we were sneaking away, we heard him rejoin Ares against the goddesses," Cupid said.

Hera jumped to her feet and clutched her chest. "Oh, my dear gods!"

Everyone in the room turned their eyes to their queen.

"What is it?" Hades asked.

"Hera?" Poseidon moved beside her and took her arm. "Are you under attack?"

Hera glanced around the room at all of the eager faces. "Therese is pregnant. I can feel them."

"Them?" Than leapt from his chair to her side. "You can sense Therese, too?"

"No," Hera said. "Not Therese. Your twins. Therese is pregnant with twins."

Than fell to his knees before Hera. "Can you save them?" He hoped beyond hope her answer was yes.

Hera gazed down at him with kind eyes. Never in his ancient history had the Olympian queen been kind to him. He hoped that, if it were to happen only once, it would be to help him save his family.

Hera said, "If Zeus swallows them, they will continue to grow inside of him, just as Athena did. And maybe we can bind him again and rescue them all."

Than doubted that the third time would be the charm in this instance. If Zeus swallowed Therese and his babies, the Alliance would have to trick him somehow, some way. He couldn't give up. It had taken

Athena centuries, though. How long would it take him? *Dear gods*, he prayed.

Hera continued, "But…"

Than's heart seemed to stop altogether. "But what?"

"If he cuts her up into pieces," Hera said, "which would be stupid, since…"

"Wait," Than said. "That's it. We *want* him to cut her up, right? As painful as that would be—and I know firsthand—it's a way out of this mess. Her soul will call to me, and nothing will hold me back! I'll disintegrate into the hundreds and overtake Zeus and his allies. I'll save Therese and our babies and help the Alliance!"

Just as Than jumped to his feet with renewed hope, Hera put a hand on his shoulder and said, "But if Therese dies, you will lose the twins."

He froze. "What? Why? Aren't they immortal?"

*Two, but none immortal.*

"Gods don't become immortal until they are born," Persephone explained as she put an arm around Than. "That's why Zeus tried to kill Melinoe while she was still in my womb."

Than wanted to scream, but when his words came out, they were low and coarse, as though his throat had constricted into a tiny tube. "That's what the Fates meant!" he said to his open, trembling hands as every world ever created dropped out from under him. "Oh my gods, Zeus is going to destroy my babies before they're even born!"

"Calm down," Hades commanded him.

He wanted his brother. *Hypnos!*

Hip appeared beside him in an instant. Than reported everything to his brother, who propped him up at the shoulders.

How many times had he taken the souls of tiny babies before they were born? Now that it was happening to him, he couldn't stand it. Never before had he understood with greater clarity what it was like to be a man.

*Two, but none immortal.*

Even if he could save Therese, he couldn't save their babies.

All hope was lost.

***

Hypnos listened to his brother brief him on the latest. As he did his best to console Than in the Underworld, promising him that they would do everything in their power to save Therese and their babies, back in Apollo's chariot, he turned to the god of light and shared Than's story.

"This is grave indeed," Apollo said as they plowed through the clouds toward Helios.

Hip disintegrated once again and found Artemis and Amphitrite swimming the seven seas, recruiting the water nymphs of the world. He relayed Than's story to them.

"We have no time to lose," Artemis said.

Gods and goddesses came out of the woodwork to hear Hip tell Than's story, and one after another was moved to join the Athena Alliance. Three sons from Poseidon came:  Aeolus, that wind bag, flew over from the Himalayas; Proteus and Triton came from the sea along with their sisters, Rhode and Kym. Briareos, Kym's husband, blew in from the Arctic, and Rhode was joined by her husband, Helios, who brightened the Underworld more than it had ever been.

Rhode, who was also a daughter of Aphrodite, convinced her brother Anteros and her sister Harmonia to join them. Apollo's sons Asklepios and Aristaios also appeared, ready for battle. They were followed by the daughters of Hephaestus. Soon, many chambers of the Underworld were filled with gods and goddesses ready to charge Mount Olympus to demand justice from their king.

No doubt others flocked to Mount Olympus to side with Zeus.

As the members of the Athena Alliance prepared their attack, Poseidon asked Hip to wake Cybele, to ask if she was strong enough to help. With some hesitation, the god of sleep blew a waking breath on the mother of the Olympians and waited as she opened her eyes and stretched her limbs.

"How long was I sleeping?" the manly goddess asked.

"Twelve hours, Mother," Hera replied before Hip could get the words out himself.

"We have assembled a massive army." Hades bent over Cybele. "We are preparing to charge Mount Olympus, where Zeus has imprisoned Therese and threatened to swallow her."

"Don't forget Hestia," Persephone said.

"Yes," Cybele said. "I foresaw all you describe."

What? Hip turned to find his brother pushing through the crowd to the bed.

"Do you foresee what will become of Therese and our babies?" Than asked gently but urgently. Sweat beaded on Than's forehead, and his chest rose and fell in rapid succession.

"My visions are hazy," Cybele replied. "But I do see a great sacrifice done out of love. I cannot see whose."

Hip wished he could silence the manly goddess for his brother's sake, for he could tell by the look on Than's face that his brother believed the sacrifice would be Therese.

***

Therese watched in horror as Zeus went from room to room and ordered the remaining gods and goddesses on Mount Olympus to assemble in the great hall. Pasithea and Thalia clung to one another beside Ares, clearly frightened out of their minds. Hestia's maidens crouched in fear behind the two Graces near the dining room door. The Muses held hands in a single line in front of Apollo's throne. A group of satyrs stood firmly at the side of Hermes, not far from the forge. Two tiny sea nymphs crept from Poseidon's chambers and stood, quaking, near the sea god's throne.

"No one leaves," Zeus bellowed. "And no one gets in."

One of the Seasons, either Eunomia or Eirene (Therese wasn't sure which), flitted into the room and announced, "Visitors claiming to be allies are demanding entrance outside the gates."

"Do not let them in," Zeus commanded. "It could be a trap. No one enters. No one leaves. Not until I've eaten the goddess of animal companions."

Therese's mouth was dryer than a field in drought. When she tried to swallow, her tight and scratchy throat had no salve. Her bleeding had stopped, thanks to Hestia's bandage, but she was still light-headed and terrified. She knew at this moment she would be better off dead than alive. She prayed to Hermes.

*Slice off my head. Make it quick. I beg of you, Lord Hermes. If we were ever friends, if you ever loved me, I beg of you to kill me now.*

"I'm glad to know there are things about me you like, Therese," Zeus said. "Because you will be spending eternity with me." He pointed to his belly. "Right here."

*Please, Hermes. I will be your servant all my days. Spare me this fate.*

"Who knows?" Zeus continued. "Like Metis, you may grow to love me. And like the goddess of wisdom, you might even make a fine advisor."

Zeus grew closer. Every nerve in Therese's body twitched. Every muscle flinched. Every bone was as cold as ice, even while her dry, tight throat was on fire.

Zeus opened his great mouth and leaned over her.

Therese closed her eyes, but just before her lids shielded her sight, she saw Hermes grab his sword, and as she squeezed her lids tightly closed, she prayed once more to him.

*Do it now!*

She waited with her eyes shut tight, but no sword fell across her neck. Nor did Zeus envelope her with his mouth. She dared to peek at the scene before her.

At Zeus's feet tumbled the bloody head of Hermes, and in the flailing, headless body across the hall, Hermes's hand still held the sword that had severed it.

## CHAPTER TWENTY

# Stalemate

Thanatos and the rest of the Athena Alliance flew across the sky in dozens of chariots toward Mount Olympus, ready to storm the gates. They weren't surprised to find an army loyal to the king defending the fortress on the outside. Heartless Nike, the goddess of victory and daughter to Ares, hovered beside her brother, Enyalios, another war god. They both held long spears in each hand. Palaistra, Hermes's daughter and the goddess of wrestling, hovered beside them, and behind this trio were Keto and Phorcys and their monstrous daughters Scylla and Echidna, the half nymph and half snake. Than found it ironic that the old man of the sea wouldn't help him and Apollo save Athena, but he seemed all too eager to defend the gates of Olympus for King Zeus.

The loyal army had no chance against the band of rebels Athena had amassed. Even horrible Scylla hesitated in raising her pincers against the sheer multitude of gods and goddesses on Than's side.

"Move away from the gate!" Hades demanded.

Athena lifted her spear. "We seek justice, not defeat!"

"Get back, you traitors!" the son of Ares shouted in reply.

No one gave the order to charge, but Alecto and Meg flew like bullets past the front line and directly for Enyalios. Their hair hissed and the blood dripped onto their victim in a foul mess. Artemis followed their lead and took down Palaistra. Poseidon and Amphitrite pummeled over the old man of the sea and his wife, making Scylla shriek. But soon both Scylla and her sister were tied in the iron chains of Hades and de-mobilized with the paralyzing sting of Poseidon's trident.

Before the conflict was resolved, Than felt a soul calling to him from the inside of the court. He naturally disintegrated, and, like a magnet, flew through the gate. The four Seasons gawked at him, but did nothing as he passed. A horrible feeling in the pit of his stomach made him mourn the death of his twins before he laid eyes on the soul beckoning to him.

It was Hermes.

Now it was Than's turn to gawk.

*Hermes?* Than whispered to the soul of his cousin as he took in the scene. Therese was chained to Zeus's throne with Hestia beside her, arms up in a protective posture against Zeus, who stood stunned at the sight of his son's head at his feet. Than realized he had little time to act, and if he was to save his family, he must act now. He disintegrated into the hundreds.

As one of him left with the soul of Hermes, the remaining hundreds pinned Zeus to the ground and trampled down the gates, allowing the other members of the Athena Alliance to enter.

To Hermes, Than said, "Why did you do it?"

Hermes stammered a bit, looking disoriented, but when Than put his hand on his cousin's shoulder, the messenger god seemed to regain his presence of mind.

"I felt the baby," Hermes said. "When I was chaining Therese, the baby kicked me."

"Babies," Than said with a grin as a wave of emotions swept over him.

"Huh?" They neared Charon's raft.

"Twins," Than explained as he guided his cousin aboard.

"Well, now."

"You saved their lives, cousin." Than looked away to hide his tears from the other god. He watched Charon drag the long pole through the river as he'd done for centuries. "Did it hurt?"

"The kick from the baby?"

Than stifled a smile. "No, the…" He drew his index finger across his throat.

"I can't remember."

Than grinned again and patted Hermes on the back. "Good."

They followed the path past the judges, who had nothing to say of an immortal's soul, and headed straight for Tartarus.

"This is your first time down here as one of the dead, am I right?" Than asked. Hermes had never died in Than's lifetime, but his cousin was older.

"First time," Hermes said. "It's strange to be on this side of death."

Hermes had escorted the souls for hundreds of years before Thanatos took over as Death.

They followed the Phlegethon where it met the iron gate. Than dragged it open against the rock. The screech of iron on stone brought Tizzie's notice to them. She looked up from her victim, befuddled by their approach. Than explained in a brief prayer. Then he turned to Hermes.

"You won't be down here long."

They rounded a corner toward the cascading asphodel and dim orange light where the Phlegethon no longer flowed.

A figure shuffled toward them from the darkness.

Than flinched at the sight of Pete Holt. Even though he was not a corporeal presence, the sockets of his ethereal head had been emptied.

"Ah," Pete said with a strange smile. "My killer has finally arrived."

Hermes turned a fearful look toward Than. "What's this all about? I do a good deed, and I'm punished for it?"

"Funny," Pete said. "The same thing has happened to me."

"I have nothing to do with it," Than said to Hermes. "Pete, Hermes never meant to kill you. What's this about?"

"I only came to thank him," Pete said. "For saving Therese and the twins."

"You knew about them?" Than asked. "Why didn't you say something?"

"Not in time to do anything about it," Pete said.

Than didn't know what to say.

"But now that I've seen them," Pete continued, his empty sockets staring back at Than, "You can tell your father that his suspicions are right."

With eyebrows drawn together, Than shook his head. "What do you mean?"

"Your twins are *the* twins," Pete replied.

"What's that supposed to mean?" Hermes asked.

"The lord of the Underworld can tell you." Pete turned and shuffled back toward the darkness.

"Why can't you?" Thanatos demanded.

"It's your father's secret; not mine."

***

Therese watched in amazement as Than multiplied and dominated Mount Olympus. Several of him broke the chains and shackles that bound her, and one took her in his arms.

"Let's get you away from here," he said.

"No, wait."

She gingerly scooped up the head of Hermes. Than followed her lead and found the body, and together they carried the messenger god to the safety of his chambers, where they laid him out on his bed. Most of the blood had already drained. When they positioned him just so, he appeared to be sleeping.

Therese still could not believe what he'd done for her. What strength and courage it must have taken to unsheathe the sword, whip the arm around, and bear the blade against his neck. She shuddered.

Then she turned to Than and said, "I want to fight."

"But we still don't have Zeus secure," Than protested. "As I was pinning him down, he slipped a thunderbolt from his boot."

"What?" She headed for the great hall, but Than grabbed her arm.

"Let me take you to safety," he said gently. "Zeus swore on the River Styx to swallow you. I don't want to risk it."

"I can't run to safety while everyone else…"

"It's not just you I'm worried about," he said.

Therese narrowed her eyes, trying to guess his meaning, but came up with nothing.

"You're pregnant."

She clutched her belly. "I'm what?"

He pulled her into his arms. "We're having twins."

Her jaw dropped and she searched his eyes, looking from one to the other. Was he telling her the truth? Was she really pregnant with twins?

"Please let me take the three of you to safety before things get worse."

Tears sprang to her eyes and she nodded. "Okay." For the sake of the babies, she supposed she would have to go.

They god travelled directly to their rooms, where he carried her to bed.

"Stay here with me for as long as possible," he said.

She snuggled against him. "Tell me what's happening. Why can't the Alliance take Zeus into their custody?"

"He's taken a hostage."

Her body stiffened. "Who?"

He didn't reply. Instead, he covered her mouth with his, and clutched her in his hands, and this was all the answer she needed.

Zeus had Than.

He loved her like it was the last time.

***

Hypnos staggered back, butting up against the door to the forge. Zeus held Than in a head lock with one arm, and he gripped a thunderbolt at the end of the other.

"I'll paralyze him for all eternity if anyone moves," the king of the gods barked.

"And I'll do the same to Ares," Poseidon roared.

Everyone turned to see Poseidon with his trident directed at Ares while three Thans held the god of war still.

No one moved.

Hypnos looked from Poseidon to Zeus. The nostrils of both gods flared. Their faces, equally red with rage, looked like demons. Except for the rapid rise and fall of their chests, they stood like statues.

The voice of Hades reverberated throughout the hall, but Hip could not see the source of it.

"We are at a stalemate, brothers," Hades said. "I wear the helm and could easily unhand you of your thunderbolt, brother, but I want to offer a compromise."

Hip held his breath, wondering how Zeus would respond.

Hera fell on her knees before Zeus. "Please, my lord. Listen to what Hades has to say."

"My heart still pains from the sting of your betrayal!" Zeus growled.

"You left me behind!" Hera said through tears. "You managed to save the others."

"Your room was the furthest from me. One of the Furies discovered me before I could get to you. I came back for you, but you had already lost faith in me."

This would not bode well, Hip thought as he studied Hera's face. The corners of her mouth were pulled down so low that she resembled the mask of tragedy. He'd seen her frown a million times, but never had it been so deep.

"It doesn't matter," Hades interrupted. "Hera has already sworn to support the Athena Alliance. She wants her equal portion as ruler of the skies and leader of the gods."

Zeus narrowed his eyes. "Is this true, Hera?"

Hera climbed to her feet and wiped the tears with the back of her hand. "Every word of it. I love you, but I despise some of the choices you have made. I want you to swear an oath."

"Not that long ago, you wanted to destroy Thanatos and his sweetheart over an apple, and now you've sworn an oath to serve with them?" Zeus scoffed.

Hera put her hands on her slender hips and dared to walk closer to the king of the gods. "Do you know why my apples mean so much to me? Do you?"

"Because they give immortality to all who eat them," Zeus said in a matter-of-fact tone. "And you want to hoard that power from the other gods. I don't blame you. I am the only god who can grant immortality to a person through the consumption of ambrosia. You want your way, too."

Tears fell from Hera's eyes and slid down her cheeks. "You are wrong, husband." Her voice was sad and quiet. "I love my apples because they were a wedding gift to me from Gaia. The day I accepted you as my husband, she planted the tree. She told me that as long as it had apples hanging from its branches, your love for me would live; but if a day came when there were no more apples hanging from its leaves, that would be the day your heart would turn cold to me."

Zeus's eyes widened and then his face grew tender. For once since Hip had known Zeus, the lord of the gods appeared speechless.

The voice of Hades, still invisible beneath his helm, broke the silence. "Does the tree still bear apples?"

"It does," Hera replied. "But I'm afraid Gaia was wrong. My lord no longer loves me, or he would hear what I have to say."

"Am I not listening to you now?" Zeus said. He continued to hold Than in a head lock and did not drop his thunderbolt, but his face had softened and his nostrils no longer flared.

Hera moved even closer to the king, so that less than five feet remained between them. "You have been faithful to me for many years."

"Indeed, I have."

"And you were afraid to set Metis free, because of the prophecy."

"Not afraid. I wanted to act wisely. I wanted to protect the order of Mount Olympus from an old Titan threat. But Athena would not rest."

Hera crossed her arms at her chest. "So, you hatched a plan to trick her."

"No one was supposed to get hurt."

"Except for Melinoe and Cybele," Persephone said.

"Not Cybele."

"Melinoe," Hera said.

Hip regretted every malicious thing he'd ever said about his sister. She had become a monstrous villain to the human race, but he realized that he might have, too, if his own father had misshapen him in the womb and then deceived and betrayed him his entire life.

Zeus averted his eyes. "Yes. Look what she has become."

"Do you not see your hand in her fate?" Persephone questioned.

"Yes. And by sentencing her to Tartarus, I would have righted another wrong."

"No!" Persephone cried.

*Please, Mother,* Hip warned. *Stay out of it for now.* Hip did not want Zeus on the defensive. Hera was handling it well. He worried his mother's accusatory tone would spoil the discussion.

"We have to give our daughter the chance to redeem herself!" Persephone cried.

Hera turned a vicious face to Persephone and shouted, "Back down!"

*Please, Mother.* Hip repeated. *For gods' sakes.*

"What is it you want from me?" Zeus demanded.

"I want to be your equal partner, your co-ruler," Hera said.

Zeus grinned, a soft chuckle escaping his lips. The chuckle erupted into full-blown laughter.

Hera looked about to attack. "What's so funny?"

Zeus regained control of himself and said, "Dear, Hera. You already are. Don't you realize the control you have over me? I'm constantly looking over my back, hoping not to displease you. You know how to make me suffer, do you not? You withhold your affection or dole it out to me, and in so doing, you make me your puppet. How can you stand there and demand from me something you already possess?"

It was Hera's turn to be speechless. Metis quickly stepped forward to Hera's side.

"Lord Zeus, we ask that the mothers and daughters in general be given equal treatment."

"How are they not given it already?" Zeus said in a tone that was not unfriendly.

"You drew lots with your brothers and disregarded your sisters," Metis clarified. "You cast your mother aside. You misused your daughter."

"I ask again," he said, his temper flaring. "What would you have me do? Be specific!"

Athena stepped forward. "You and Hera rule the sky. Poseidon and Amphitrite co-rule the sea. Hades and Persephone co-rule the Underworld. Allow Demeter and Hestia to co-rule the land and its inhabitants."

Demeter was not present, but Hestia covered her mouth with her hands.

"They are your sisters and rightful heirs, like you," Athena said. "Demeter already takes care of the lands, and Hestia watches over the households of mortals."

"Also, Metis and Cybele must remain free," Artemis added.

"And given positions of honor in this court," Amphitrite added.

"Yes," Athena agreed. "My mother can continue to be your advisor, but here, where she can be acknowledged."

"And you must swear on the River Styx to overturn your previous oath to swallow Therese," Hades added, still invisible to all.

"If I am to consider your demands, you must all agree to my conditions, too," Zeus said.

"What conditions?" Poseidon asked, his trident still pointed at Ares.

"All must swear to never make another human immortal. No more apotheosis to upset the balance of our pantheon."

Hip winced. If the gods agreed, then Jen would never join him as one of the gods.

"Is that it?" Hades asked.

"Hera must make every god and goddess incapable of further reproduction," Zeus declared. "To further protect the balance."

Hera lifted her chin. "But Therese is already pregnant."

Zeus gazed across the room at the Thans holding the arms of Ares. "Is this true?"

Before Than could reply, Hera said, "With twins."

Zeus cleared his throat. "No. You must agree that they cannot be immortal like the rest of us. Demigod, yes. Immortal, no."

Hip met his brother's eyes. Than and Therese would have to watch their children die mortal deaths. Hip wondered if Than would be the one to escort the souls of his own children to Charon's raft. Sadness gripped his heart.

"Why not enforce your demand after the twins are born?" Persephone asked.

"Because the gods of the Underworld are too powerful already," Zeus growled. "The power of disintegration of your twins leaves me no choice but to demand a stop to the creation of more allies of the house of Hades."

"Fair enough," Hades said.

"Do you have any further demands?" Athena asked.

"I want your love and forgiveness," Zeus said. "But I cannot demand it of you. I never meant to hurt you, Athena, but only to protect my kingdom. I still fear that Metis will bear a child that will destroy me."

"So, you *are* afraid," Hera said.

"Does that bring you happiness?" Zeus challenged.

"Somewhat, because it makes me love you all the more," she replied. "It's harder to love someone who has no vulnerabilities."

Hip noticed that Hera did indeed have a way of controlling Zeus. His demeanor softened and his tight hold on Than seemed to relax.

"If we gods are rendered sterile, then you have nothing to fear from my mother," Athena reasoned.

"Prophecies are only predictions," Apollo added. "Unlike an edict from the Fates, they are never a guarantee but are only realized on condition."

Zeus seemed to consider this. Hip held his breath and glanced around the room. All eyes except for Poseidon's (who kept his trident steadily on Ares) were focused on the king.

"I will agree to your terms if you will agree to mine," Zeus said. "We must all swear on the River Styx to uphold all that was stated."

The faces of the gods in the Athena Alliance transformed into the smiling faces of victors. Everyone swore at the same time. Zeus lowered his thunderbolt and released Than. Poseidon lowered his trident. The war was over. Order had been restored.

Now that he could, Hip thought only of Jen and wondered what kind of future, if any, they had together.

CHAPTER TWENTY-ONE

# The Gatekeeper's Secret

Than fell on his back in bed as his heart rate returned to normal and his body relaxed. He hadn't realized how tense he had been until now that the conflict was over. While the gods congratulated one another on Mount Olympus, Than wiped the sweat from his brow with the back of his arm and sighed with relief beside his wife.

As if she sensed a change in his mood, Therese curled against him. "You okay?"

"Zeus has agreed to our terms."

Therese sat up beside him, squealing with excitement. "That's wonderful! Oh, Than!"

He looked up at her smiling face as it bent down to kiss him again. Her bright red hair fanned around his face and tickled his chin. When she sat back up, she frowned.

"What's wrong?" she asked him.

He hadn't realized he'd given anything away. He had been hoping to hold off the inevitable conversation to bask in the glow of victory with his wife a little while longer.

"Zeus made counter-demands."

***

Jen strapped Lynn into a seatbelt beside her on the bench seat of her truck and drove her up the road to the Bradshaw house.

"Where Terry go?" Lynn asked again.

"She'll be back soon," Jen said, though she had no idea whether that was true.

When Carol answered the door, her smile faded when she noticed Therese was not among them.

"Therese had to leave suddenly," Jen lied. "I'm not sure why, but she asked me to bring Lynn home."

There was no way Jen would tell Carol the truth.

"Oh, no." Carol took Lynn by the hand. "That's too bad. I better call her. Would you like to come inside?"

"No thanks. I'm needed back home."

As she drove back down the road to her house, Jen tried once again to find out what had happened. She remembered crying out to Hip. She recalled him showing up outside her house. Then the next thing she knew, she was waking up in the family room with Bobby's foot on her lap.

"Therese? Can you hear me? What in the heck is going on?"

The morning of Pete's funeral, Jen was rummaging through her closet for her one black dress (had she had it dry cleaned after her father's funeral and never picked it up?) when she had the daylights scared out of her.

Beside her in the not-so-good light of the walk-in closet, Therese appeared.

"Oh, eem, gee, Therese!" Jen clapped a hand against her beating heart. "Don't ever do that to me again. You scared the crap out of me!"

"Sorry." Therese didn't even try to hide her grin.

"Where have you been, anyway? You've had me worried to death."

Therese frowned. "It's, um, complicated."

"Don't give me that."

"Do you mind if we get out of the closet?"

Jen huffed, full of battling emotions. On the one hand, it was the morning of her brother's freaking funeral, for crying out loud. She was a wreck. A total wreck. On the other hand, she was super relieved to see Therese.

Jen collapsed on her bean bag as Therese sat on the edge of Jen's bed.

"Well?" Jen demanded.

"Well…there was this huge conflict on Mount Olympus," Therese began. "Zeus swore to swallow me whole, so I'd be separated from Than for all eternity."

"Because of what Pete said," Jen said, feeling guilty that one of her family members had put her friend in danger. But hadn't Therese put *them* in danger? Wouldn't Pete still be alive if Therese hadn't insisted on marrying Than?

"It might have happened the way it did regardless," Therese said. "But it's over now, so I'm no longer in danger, and I could finally come to see you. I came as soon as I could, I hope you know."

Jen felt the blood rush to her face. She should have known Therese had a reason for being gone so long. "I know."

"I haven't even seen Carol and Richard and Lynn yet. I came straight here."

"Are you going to the funeral?"

"Of course." Therese fiddled with her gray blazer.

"That's a killer blazer by the way," Jen said.

"Thanks. Anyway, before we go, I wanted to tell you a couple of things."

"What?" Jen bit her bottom lip. Maybe Therese had news about Hip. Did Jen even want to hear it?

"First of all, Pete is in the Underworld, and he's actually doing really well. He told me to tell you hi. I think he and Tizzie might have a thing for one another."

"Okay, this is weird." Jen jumped up from the bean bag and paced the room. "You're freaking me out."

"Does that mean you couldn't handle going to see him?"

Jen's mouth dropped open. What was Therese saying? "Are you serious? When? How?"

Therese clutched her abdomen, like she was going to be sick.

"You alright?" Jen asked, alarmed.

"Yeah, fine." Therese smiled. "Hip got Hades to agree to let you come down for a visit."

Jen stared at Therese. Did she have any idea how odd that sounded? Anyone else overhearing their conversation might think they were talking about an ordinary visit. "Go down for a visit? Therese, this sounds crazy. When? How would it work?" And would Hip be there? she wondered.

"I don't know when exactly," Therese said. "But soon. Either I or Hip would take you—your choice."

"My choice?"

"Hip isn't sure how you feel about him," Therese explained.

Jen fell back on the bean bag chair. She wasn't sure, either. "Yeah."

"So think about it," Therese added. "Meanwhile, I have other news."

The look on Therese's face—it was beaming, glowing.

"Oh my god," Jen said. "You're pregnant."

"With twins."

Jen jumped back up. "Twins?"

Therese jumped up, too. "Can you believe it?"

"Wow. Congrats. Two baby gods."

Therese's smile turned into a frown. "Well, not gods. Demigods. They'll have special powers, but they'll be mortal."

Jen didn't really know much about the gods, but she was pretty sure that when one god got pregnant by another, the result was another god—or in this case, twin gods. Maybe the fact that Therese was not born of a god made it different for her.

"How will they live in the Underworld if they aren't gods?"

Therese shrugged. "Don't know."

"Will they be able to be around Than without dying, or Hip without falling asleep?"

"We won't know until they're born." Therese sank back down on the bed.

"I'm sorry," Jen said, realizing she was asking too many hard questions. "I didn't mean…"

"No. It's okay."

Jen sat beside Therese and put an arm around her friend. She felt warm, like a mortal. In fact, sometimes Jen wondered if all that had happened with Therese and Hip hadn't been one long, weird dream.

They sat there quietly for a few minutes. Then Therese broke the silence and asked, "Does this mean you've forgiven me for what happened with Pete?"

Jen cocked her head to one side. Had she forgiven Therese? "Sort of. It's been hard. I still can't believe he's gone. I mean, is he gone?"

"Yes and no," came Therese's cryptic reply.

"Whatever that means."

"Can I ride with you to the funeral?"

Jen noticed tears in Therese's eyes. "Of course."

***

A few days after Pete's funeral, Therese was out on a mission on Stormy's back helping a lost litter of kittens when she heard Than calling to her.

*Come back as soon as you can.*

*Has something happened? Is it an emergency?* Therese replied. It wasn't yet time for his visit from the Maenads—that was in early August.

*No, no. Nothing like that. Just something my father wants to tell us. It has to do with the twins.*

As soon as Therese had helped the kittens to find their mother and home, Therese returned to the Underworld. She found Than pacing before the hearth.

"Ready?" he asked when she entered.

"I guess so. What's this about?" she asked as he took her hand and they god travelled to his father's rooms.

Once in Hades's sitting room, Than whispered, "Apparently there is a prophecy about our twins."

Therese's stomach did a flip flop—or maybe it was the two growing babies. Hera had told her it was a girl and a boy, and she and Than had agreed they would be called Hermes and Hestia, after the gods who had saved their lives. Hera had also explained that demigods tended to grow more quickly in the womb than regular mortal babies, and they were more rambunctious. She had warned Therese that she would feel quite a bit of movement, and Hera hadn't been wrong. Therese clutched the swelling pooch that was now her abdomen and took a seat beside Than.

Hades lifted his head from the book he'd been reading. "Good. You're here."

"So what did Pete mean when he said to tell you that these are *the* twins?" Than asked.

Therese had no idea what Than was talking about. "Pete said what?"

Than caught her up on what had happened. "I was waiting until the right moment to tell you," he explained.

Hades crossed one leg over the other and leaned on an elbow while he picked at his beard. "Long ago, before I met your mother, I was walking along a field of asphodel in the Upperworld wearing my helm of invisibility while praying to Aphrodite to help me find a bride. I was lonesome, and at that time, I found my work and my lot to be loathsome."

Therese glanced at Than to see him listening intently to his father. She sucked in her lips, full of anxiety as she protectively cupped her abdomen. No matter what, she would protect her babies. It didn't matter what the prophecy was. Apollo once told her that only the Fates knew the certain future. Everyone else had visions that could change.

"The Fates made a deal with me," Hades continued.

Therese's heart sank. "The Fates?"

"Yes," Hades said. "You see, at that time, they lived on Mount Olympus, but their lives were more loathsome than mine. They begged me for both protection and a diversion. So I set them up here under my protection and built them their little casino to keep them occupied."

"I never knew they lived anywhere else," Than said.

"This was such a long time before you were born," Hades explained. "In exchange for this favor, the Fates told me to choose my bride wisely, and they pointed me in the direction of Persephone, who was, one day, wandering among the same asphodel. The Fates promised me that when the minds of men had come to forget the gods and to lose their love for one another, the seed of my seed, a set of twins, one boy and one girl, would go into the world of men and restore their faith in both the gods and in one another."

Therese's eyebrows shot up. "Do you mean to say…?"

She looked at Than, whose mouth hung open in half-smile and half-shock, speechless.

"If Pete is right," Hades said. "If your twins are *the* twins—and believe me, I always thought Hypnos would be the first to marry and have children, so I didn't see this coming—then one day they will make us very proud. They will become beacons of hope for all of humanity."

"But how?" Therese asked.

"That is for the Fates to know and for us to find out," Hades replied.

Therese turned to Than, whose smile stretched from ear to ear. Tears welled in his eyes. She wanted to kiss him. Never before this moment had she ever been happier.

THE END

Thank you for reading my story. I hope you enjoyed it. If you did, please consider leaving a review. Reviews help readers to find my books, which helps me.

Please enjoy the first chapter from the next book, *Hades's Promise.*

CHAPTER ONE

# A Short Honeymoon

The shifting hues of the Aurora Borealis danced above Therese as she lay with Than on a blanket on the frosty summit of Mount Thor—home of the world's greatest vertical drop. For their honeymoon, Than had brought her to Baffin Island in Northern Canada near the North Pole. The light show lasted several minutes until Helios appeared, bright and early at two in the morning. His golden cup would remain visible for a good twenty hours, which was precisely the reason Than had brought Therese to this spot.

She kissed the side of his face. "Spectacular," she whispered.

"I thought you'd like it." He pulled her more closely into him as the rays from Helios enveloped them in the sunrise. "It's the brightest place on Earth, next to Mount Olympus."

And the opposite of the Underworld in every way. Why did he still think she didn't love the house of Hades? Not wanting to hurt his feelings, she thanked him again and snuggled closer to him.

He yawned lazily. She rarely saw him so peaceful-looking.

They'd ridden polar bears, sang with narwhals, swam with baby penguins, and sunbathed with walruses. Than had thought of everything she'd enjoy. Therese felt like the luckiest person in the world.

Now it was cuddle time beneath the fantastic northern lights, which were fading in Helios's beams.

A movement near her ribs made her flinch. The babies were waking up.

"He's up high today," she said of the boy twin inside her.

"How do you know it's Hermes and not Hestia?"

"I sense them." She lifted his hand toward her swollen belly. "Maybe you can sense them, too."

He laid his large hand, with its thick, long fingers, up against her skin and waited. His eyes suddenly widened with surprise.

"Hestia! I can't explain how I know it's her!" His face beamed.

And he'd never looked sexier.

"Pretty amazing, huh?" She winked.

"She put her tiny baby hand up to mine," he said, astounded.

"They aren't like regular mortal babies, are they," she said without inflection. "They're so advanced."

"They *are* demigods."

"I can't wait to hold them in my arms."

He frowned.

"I'm sorry." She clapped her hand to her forehead. "I'm so stupid." She kept forgetting how he must feel, knowing he would endanger the lives of their children if he was in their presence once they were born.

"We should have a plan." The muscle near his jaw flexed.

She sat up and leaned over him. "We'll ask Hip to switch with you, just until the twins become adults—eighteen years tops. That's nothing to him, right?"

"It's a lot to ask."

"You could offer to give him breaks every day."

Than gave her a half smile. "But I'd still never see the twins awake."

"You could hold them in your arms as they slept."

"Maybe he'd do it—switch with me."

"I think he would. He loves you so much. So stop worrying, okay?" She leaned down and kissed him.

She could sense in the way he kissed her back that he was worried. Hermes and Hestia may never have the chance to get to know their father.

"A-hem," came an unexpected voice nearby.

The newlyweds turned their heads to find Dionysus, in nothing but a loin cloth, standing over them.

"Sorry to interrupt," he said. "But the Maenads are waiting."

***

Than was surprised to find that Dionysus had led them to Crete, near the palace ruins of Knossos.

"What's going on?" Therese asked.

"The Maenads have grown fond of the Minotaur and his labyrinth," Dionysus said.

Ariadne appeared with a scowl. "How many times must I ask you to call him by his Greek name? Is that so difficult?"

Dionysus turned to see his estranged wife glaring at him. "My apologies. Old habits."

"Make new ones," Ariadne said. Then she took Therese by the hands and asked, "How are you holding up?"

Than knew Therese was trying to be brave for him, as always. This was harder on her than it was on him.

Asterion emerged from the labyrinth followed by three Maenads and two Curetes.

"What, Curetes, too?" Than asked of the dancing men and their crashing cymbals.

"They heard the Maenads and came down from the mountain," Dionysus explained.

"They were just leaving," Asterion added. "Go on, men. Now's not a good time."

The Curetes skipped away in a rush of clangs and hops.

"I don't like this," Ariadne said to Dionysus. "I told you I didn't want this here."

"Asterion's never been happier," the god of the vine objected. "You said so yourself."

"The company has been good for him, but my nerves can't handle what the Maenads are about to do."

Dionysus wrapped his arms around her waist. "If we're to be together…"

"It doesn't matter," Than interrupted. "Let's just get it over with. The sooner the better."

***

Jen stopped outside the master bedroom door, her heart aching at the sound of her mother's sobs. She couldn't take the sorrow anymore. Jen had to tell her.

She tapped on the door and went in. "Mom?"

Her mother lay on her bed, hugging her pillow. Her whole body shook, but she stopped as soon as she heard Jen come in.

"Oh, hi there, sweet baby girl. Don't mind me." She wiped her swollen eyes with the bed sheet. "I'm such a mess."

"That's alright, Mom." Jen sat on the edge of the bed with one leg curled underneath her. "Maybe if you just got out more. It's too bad Mr. Stern hasn't come around in a while."

More tears poured from Mrs. Holt's eyes. "I just haven't been in any kind of shape for company lately."

"You haven't come out to help with the horses for three days."

"I'm not feeling well, baby doll."

"Remember when Dumbo died?"

"'Course I do." She wiped her face with the sheet. "Why do you ask?"

"You made Therese come help with the horses the very next day."

"I wouldn't say I *made* her."

Jen picked at the bed covers. "You pressured her enough."

"Now, listen here, baby girl." Her mother's face turned red. "You can't compare the loss of Dumbo to your brother. And I *was* out there the very next day. We all were. I'm just not well right now."

"Mom, I'm just saying…" What *was* she trying to say? Everything seemed to be coming out all wrong. "Never mind. There's something I want to tell you. Now don't freak out."

Her mother sat up on the bed, alarmed. "Oh, no. What?"

"It's not bad. It's good. Just promise not to freak out."

"How can I promise that if I don't know what it is?"

"You know how Pete used to say Daddy's ghost talked to him?"

"Pete was sick. He couldn't help it."

"We saw Daddy's ghost that one time, too. The night he died. Remember when we were all in your tub 'cause you thought a tornado was coming? Therese convinced us it was a dream."

"Now wait a minute…" Her mother pulled the covers back and moved to the edge of the bed.

"Just listen. This is gonna sound crazy." Jen was scared to death she was doing the wrong thing. Her mother would probably think Jen was sick, like Pete. But Jen couldn't take another day of her mother's pain. "I've been to the other side. Don't freak out."

Her mother looked exasperated. "What are you talking about, baby doll?"

"It wasn't a dream, either." Jen stood up and walked around to the side of the bed to get closer to her mom. "I went to the other side, and I saw Pete."

***

Hip made his way down the deepest path of the Underworld, determined to ask Pete's advice. The seer was already condemned, so what harm could come from using his gifts? Hip's heart was hurting, and maybe Pete could tell him what to do.

Wouldn't it be just Hip's luck that the moment he knew he was one hundred percent in love, it would be with a mortal, and it would be just at the moment the lord of the gods decreed there would be no more apotheosis? If humans couldn't become gods, how would he and Jen get their happily ever after?

Before he reached the iron gate of Tartarus, he sensed Pete and Tizzie down in the seers' pit, among the asphodel where the Phlegethon did not flow. Tizzie's wolf lay at her feet. Hip was still several yards from them, and Tizzie and Pete did not seem aware of Hip's presence.

"How can I not warn them?" Pete asked in a strained, almost tortured voice.

"The visions of seers aren't guaranteed," Tizzie replied.

"You don't believe in me."

"That's not it, love. Come here."

Tizzie's dark, slender arms wrapped around Pete's transparent neck, but fell through. She struggled with the illusion of embracing him. Her long, dark, serpentine curls lay limp without their usual animation.

Tizzie sensed him then and said in an annoyed tone, "Can we help you, Hip?"

"Let's ask him what to do," Pete said.

Hip opened the gate, scratching the iron against the rock, and then closed it behind him. He made his way past the flames of the Phlegethon, turned the dark corner, and went down, down into the deep pit of the seers.

"Hey, sis," Hip said in the most nonchalant voice he could muster. "What's up?"

"Everything," she said without humor. "This *is* the Underworld."

"Double entendre?" Hip asked playfully. "I mean, everything *is* up above us, and the Underworld *is* a hopping place, am I right?"

"If you're a frog," Pete replied.

"Ha, ha, ha. Good one." Hip snapped both thumbs in the direction of the seer.

"So tell us why you're here," Tizzie demanded, and her wolf gave one sharp bark.

"Well, I was hoping for some advice, but it sounds like *you* want the same thing from *me*."

Pete said yes at the same time Tizzie said no. The two lovers glared at one another.

"Whoa," Hip said. "I didn't mean to start a war."

"It's about the twins," Pete said. "Therese's twins."

"What about them?" Therese asked from around the corner as she escorted Than into Tartarus.

Therese had obviously taken Than's duties as the god of death. Than didn't look so hot. It was August, which meant the Maenads.

"You okay, bro'?" Hip put a hand on Than's transparent shoulder.

"Huh?" Than gave him a blank look.

"Give him a minute," Therese said. She put her arms around her husband. "Than, Baby? Do you know who you are?"

"Speaking of babies," Pete said. "There's something…"

Tizzie cupped Pete's face in her hands, and blood dripped from her eyes. Her serpentine curls lifted up in a hiss before falling limp again. "Don't."

"What's this about?" Hip asked. "I get that it's about the twins, but what about them?"

"Do you mean *our* twins?" Than snapped to attention.

"They can't live here," Pete blurted out. "Hades neglected to tell you *that* part of the prophecy."

Therese's brows bent together, and her mouth fell open. "What are you saying?"

"The twins have to grow up among mortals if they're to fulfill their destiny," Pete replied.

As Therese and Than sought one another's eyes, Hip wondered what this would mean. Would Therese leave his brother behind and return to the Upperworld to raise their children?

## EVA POHLER

Eva Pohler is a *USA Today* bestselling author of over thirty novels in multiple genres, including mysteries, thrillers, and young adult paranormal romance based on Greek mythology. Her books have been described as "addictive" and "sure to thrill"—*Kirkus Reviews*.

To learn more about Eva and her books, and to sign up to hear about new releases, and sales, please visit her website at www.evapohler.com.